OFF-LABEL

A NOVEL

ERIC KAPLE

"Having the perfect face along with the perfect body is every young man's perfect dream."

—*Bodybuilding* magazine,
April, 1991

"You don't know what it's like to get picked on. Picked on to the point you can't take it no more."

—Mooky DeValle

"Who knows what lengths pharmaceutical companies will go to in order to protect their multi-billion-dollar crop?"

—Art Mellinger

PROLOGUE

Saturday, June 4, 1983
Pete's Cafe
New Washington, Ohio

Lexy sat in a corner booth of the tavern, nursing his Natty Light. He'd been nursing a lot of Natty Lights lately. Pete's had been known to get a little rowdy on Saturdays, just shy of twelve. But this night was pretty tame. With the exception of the annoying little boy who kept playing "Elvira" on the jukebox,

He can't be ten years old. What the hell is he doing here?

Lexy wasn't really irritated yet. People irritated Lexy. Hell, the only reason he'd stepped foot in the dump was because his ninth and last beer had set sail from the house a half hour ago. Drive-thru? Closed. Liquor store? Closed. Grocery store? You guessed it. The plan? Sit here. Get wasted. Be left the fuck alone. Walk home.

Two couples

Teenyboppers.

cut through the smoke-filled room and took their places at the mildly populated bar. A skinny bitch, a pair of pretty boys, and a chick with massive tits,

1

perfectly nestled in her tight low-cut violet blouse. Their threads were far finer than Lexy's daily uniform of jeans and a soiled white T-shirt.

He eyed them with disdain as they laughed and carried on. Probably celebrating graduation, he thought. Lexy's own graduation was just a couple years ago. But life since then hadn't been filled with laughter and celebration. Long days at the mill followed by long nights in the company of John Barleycorn pretty much consumed his existence. The waitress brought him another beer.

Three Natties later, Lexy again stared at the quartet whooping it up at the bar. The girl with the big boobs pulled out a Winston and Pretty Boy #1 dutifully lit it. Moments later he got up and walked towards the restroom. Lexy now had a clear view of her bosom.

What a rack.

He bit his lower lip unconsciously.

Lexy hated people, and that included uppity big-breasted bitches. But he also had needs. A string of one night stands had been fulfilling those needs. *Yep. I love em and I leave em alone.* And right then he needed The Girl with the Big Boobs. He decided to make his move.

He slid his slender frame out of the booth and made his way towards the bar. The Girl with the Big Boobs was startled as he angled onto the stool previously occupied by Pretty Boy #1. Her long, loosely curled brown hair and flawless pale complexion made a lovely match. But that's not what had his attention.

"Hi. I'm Lexy." His eyes-to-chest gaze was less than subtle.

"Um. Hi. I'm Jen. Look, I don't mean to be rude, but—"

"When was the last time you had your nipples sucked, Jen?" Lexy was nearly salivating.

"What?"

"I wanna suck the nectar right out of em."

"Hey, man, buzz off!" Pretty Boy #2 chimed in.

"My boyfriend's sitting there," Jen said nervously. "You should leave before he gets back."

"He's not sitting here now is he?" Lexy held his eager gaze on her chest. "I bet your boyfriend doesn't know what to do with all that."

As Jen's beau walked the corridor from the john back into the barroom, he noticed another man in his seat. A man who looked disheveled; a greaser. He also noticed that his girlfriend was no longer bubbly. She looked worried. Flustered.

"What's goin on?" he said.

"Hey, Gary, this asshole's hittin on Jen!" Pretty Boy #2 was starting to irritate Lexy.

Gary Sanderson had been in similar situations before. Jennifer Ashcroft was indeed a stunner, and she seemed to be mightily fond of flaunting her D-cups at every available opportunity. Quietly talking it out with the other party had worked for Gary in the past. Gary, Jen, and their two friends were enjoying post-graduation drinks and having a wonderful time. Gary didn't want to spoil the evening by getting kicked out of a bar due to fighting. He decided to utilize the skillful art of diplomacy. "Is that so?" Gary said. He then edged himself between Jen and Lexy and

3

whispered in his ear. "Look buddy, this is my girlfriend and you're in my seat. I don't want any trouble. Everyone's having a good time. Let's just keep it that way. Okay?"

Lexy, who appeared not to have heard the man in his ear, shifted his sights from Jen's breasts to Gary's eyes. "I think your girlfriend wants my cock. And I'm gonna give it to her," he said aloud.

Jen and her lady friend exchanged looks of horror.

"Hey man, you're gonna get your ass kicked!" Pretty Boy #2 screamed. At this point, most of the heads in Pete's were turned in their direction.

"It's okay, Reg." Gary was trying to be as cool as possible, but he started to feel a burning sensation run up his belly. He again leaned into Lexy's ear. "Look pal, I can tell you've had a lot to drink. Why don't you just go back to where you were sitting before this gets out of hand? Okay?"

"She wants a man, not a little boy. You don't have the dick to satisfy—"

Gary had had enough. He grabbed Lexy's collar with both hands and growled. Before Gary could initiate the front-door shuffle, Lexy caught him in the solar plexus with a right fist. He doubled-over immediately.

How do you like that, pretty boy?

As Lexy cocked his leg to deliver a rib-crushing kick, Reg's bottle of suds shattered over his head. The two locked up and almost instantly fell to the hardwood floor. Lexy was on top. He straddled Reg and slipped a vise-grip around his throat. Jen would later recall that the other patrons just sat there. Stupefied. No one did anything to stop it, including the bartender.

"Get off him! Get off him!" Reg's girlfriend screamed at the top of her lungs.

Reg's face was turning blue and his eyes looked like they were going to explode. Lexy continued choking him, with pursed lips and the singular goal of putting him to sleep. The Oak Ridge Boys continued playing from the jukebox.

"Get off him!" She was now digging into Lexy's neck with her previously perfect manicured nails.

Time to beat a bitch.

Lexy stood up and turned around—just in time to catch Gary's right cross, which landed squarely on his chin. He fell back stiffly and smacked his head on the unforgiving floor. Lights out.

When Lexy came to he was arrested and hand-cuffed behind the back by two local police officers. He felt nothing but rage.

"Fucking whores! Fucking pissants! I hate you all! I hate you all!"

PART ONE

DONOVAN

1

Transcript excerpt of a hearing of The President's
Commission Investigating Pharmaceutical Industry
Activities, AKA The Hamilton Commission
Thursday, May 16, 2019
Washington DC

Chairman Norm Hamilton (R-UT): The committee will come to order. This commission has discovered much regarding various practices of drug companies since the President charged the investigation several months ago. Now that expert testimony and the investigation itself is drawing to a close, we still have some topics to explore. We'll examine the diagnosis of short stature, the prescription drug Restor, and the evening of Friday, October 26 of last year: what's come to be known as the Occurrence in Harbor Light. We will now commence with the questioning of our next witness, Dr. Matthew Engle. At this time, the chair recognizes the gentlelady from Massachusetts, Miss Williams.

Senator Megan Williams (D-MA): Thank you, Mr. Chairman. Would you please state your name and professional title?

Engle: Matthew Engle, MD. I'm the chief of endocrinology at Holmes-Jewish Research Hospital, Seattle, Washington.

Williams: And, Dr. Engle, are you familiar with a medical condition known as short stature?

Engle: Yes, I've written several articles regarding the subject.

Williams: Doctor, the committee had an opportunity to look at some of your writings concerning the matter. We appreciate your objectivity and level of knowledge regarding this issue. Would you briefly state what short stature is?

Engle: Sure. First of all, the diagnosis is very controversial in and of itself. Simply stated, short stature is a height that would be considered below normal or average. The level of—

Williams: What would be considered normal height?

Engle: Exactly. That's one of the fundamental problems. The issue of average versus normal has been hotly contested within medicine for centuries. We can utilize statistics to gauge what averages are; in this case, what the average height is for a given age and gender. The question of what is normal, however, is highly debatable. The level of subjectivity about what is considered normal and abnormal height has always been contentious among physicians and researchers. In order to formulate a medical condition, and hence prescribe medication for it, the diagnosis needs to be defined, although the definitions aren't always clear. Technically, short stature refers to the height of an adult that is more than two standard deviations below the mean for the person's sex and age. In the United States, that would include men who are shorter than five feet four inches and women who are shorter than four feet eleven inches. That's the generally accepted definition. It's not universally agreed upon.

Williams: Do adults with short stature typically benefit from traditional drug therapy?

Engle: It's my conclusion that they do not. In fact, pharmaceutical interventions are aimed at children.

Williams: So basically, it's a childhood disorder that is defined with adult parameters?

Engle: Yes, ma'am. That's another of the controversies.

Williams: What are the causes of short stature?

Engle: There are several possible causes. The first can simply be family genes. Other causes include human growth hormone deficiency, malnutrition, inherited diseases, major syndromes, and the side effects of certain of drugs. It can also be idiopathic.

Williams: Idio—

Engle: Idiopathic. Shortness that has no known cause is called idiopathic short stature.

Williams: Doctor, have you had an opportunity to review the Donovan Marsden case?

Engle: Yes.

Williams: Was Donovan Marsden diagnosed with idiopathic short stature?

Engle: Yes.

Williams: I'm confused as to why short stature isn't considered a natural variation or deviation, and is instead categorized as a disorder.

Engle: Years ago, several pharmaceutical companies submitted clinical trial data to the FDA in an attempt to medicalize the condition; to have it considered a disorder.

Williams: Companies such as Braxton-Wentworth, the maker of Restor?

Engle: Yes. When something is classified as a disease or disorder, physicians can then legally prescribe medications for it...

2

Donovan Marsden made his bed after he readied himself for school. He carefully placed four stuffed animals on his baby blue comforter. Snuggled together in a perfect line just below the pillow were a green dinosaur, a goldfish, a golden retriever, and a tabby cat. Donovan had a special affection for this last one because it resembled the family's actual pet, Butterscotch. Although well in his teens, he didn't think he'd ever outgrow his animals.

The Marsden family (Joe, Nancy, Donovan, and Mikey) had been residing at 849 Maplewood Street for six years. A small, quiet house in a small, quiet neighborhood in the heterogeneous community of Harbor Light, Ohio. Harbor Light (population circa 25,000) is situated between Sandusky and Huron, and sits on the shore of Lake Erie. Lower-middle is how you could've classified the Marsden family, and lower-middle is how you could've classified Joe's management position at Midwest Mowers, a manufacturer of lawnmowers and snowblowers. Nancy slung the sweets at Harbor Light Confections.

"Donovan, Mikey, hurry up and eat your breakfast before you go," his mom said.

This particular morning was like most others. The boys gobbled down their meals (cold, sugary cereal), donned their attire for the brisk March air, saddled their backpacks, and headed out the door. Donovan doted on his little brother (who had recently turned seven) with almost motherly instinct, making sure he had all his supplies—*and don't forget your mittens.*

Both boys preferred to walk to school—save for the most inclement of weather, in which case Nancy gave them a ride—which was less than a mile away. They took the same path, basically a straight shot from the mailbox: cut across two adjoining lawns, cross Woodbine, down Perry, cross Myrtle, down Whisler, and *voila*; you're at the front door of Harbor Light High School. Harbor Light Elementary was just a stone's throw to the left. But they didn't walk together. Mikey made the trek with a group of three friends: Chad Eitle and the Johnson brothers. Mikey was quite popular among his peers and was already exhibiting leadership tendencies. Donovan, however, was a loner. With the exceptions of his stuffed animals and science books, Rodney McAllister was his only friend. And Rodney rode the bus.

Minutes after Mikey left, Donovan stuffed his blue stocking cap on his blond head, pushed his black-rimmed glasses up on his nose, and bid his mother goodbye. His solo journey to Harbor Light High was filled with caution. He was careful; wary of certain people.

He didn't want them to *hurt* him.

Kids had been *hurting* Donovan as long as he could remember. Being a very small child had its disadvantages. At his age, he could have been a sophomore instead of a freshman. Joe and Nancy had delayed his enrollment into grade school a year, hoping that Donovan would be closer in size to his classmates. It didn't work. He'd endured the verbal taunts over the years:

How's the air down there, pipsqueak?—among the tame

Watch where you're goin, you little four-eyed faggot!—among the harsh

He tried to ignore them, but they still stung. The *physical* bullying, however, could not be ignored. The countless times he'd had his books knocked out of his hands. The equally countless times he had gotten anonymously tripped in a crowded hallway. There was the afternoon when Brett Nelson had taken Donovan's glasses off in the restroom and crushed them under his foot (Donovan had lied to his teacher and parents and said that he had accidentally broken them on the playground). Oh, and the time when a cluster of teenage thugs had been hanging out at the corner of Woodbine and Perry after school. Donovan had tried to take a detour on his way home, in order to avoid them.

He wasn't fast enough.

Shawn Atkins grabbed Donovan by the collar and said, "I gotta special treat for ya, bitch." At which point he'd forced him to the ground and shoved his face in dogshit. Just a few of the highlights of Donovan Marsden's childhood.

Today, Donovan had an appointment with his family doctor. He'd be introduced to something that would dramatically change his life in the months to come. In the meantime, the bullying was about to get worse.

Much worse.

3

"There's a new drug on the market for ISS," Dr. Alec Wilde said to Joe, Nancy, and Donovan Marsden from behind his desk. "It's called Restor."

When Donovan had failed to assimilate with his younger classmates in the height category, Joe and Nancy had started to worry. Well, Nancy had worried. Joe had panicked. They'd consulted with their family physician, Dr. Wilde, several times regarding the issue. The good doctor had reassured them that things would likely speed up when Donovan hit puberty. He did. Things didn't. That's when Donovan's diagnosis had lengthened from short stature to idiopathic short stature.

"Now I know we've discussed therapies for this in the past: things like human growth hormone, insulin-like growth factor, and testosterone. Each of those individually tend to generate insufficient results, and the cost is astronomical, sometimes at around fifty thousand a year."

"What!" Joe yelled.

"Yeah," Dr. Wilde said. "There's a saying for some things. 'You get a lot of bang for your buck.' Only in this case, there's very little bang and a whole lotta buck."

"Doctor," Nancy started, "what's this Res—"

"Restor. Pronounced like Chester. It's a subcutaneous, combination drug. It's injected under the skin with an instrument that looks like a pen. Donovan, that means you would give yourself daily shots in your tummy. Instead of utilizing a single active ingredient, it combines several components. Given the cases I've reviewed from what one of Restor's reps has shown me, it appears to be working amazingly. Funny thing is, the drug wasn't designed for idiopathic short stature. It's prescribed off-label."

"Off-label?" Joe inquired.

"Yes," Dr. Wilde said, "the drug's sole indication is to treat severe burns. It was first used with American soldiers who suffered third-degree burns overseas. The results were incredible. Somewhere down the line, it was discovered that Restor worked extraordinarily well with idiopathic short stature. Restor's manufacturer, Braxton-Wentworth Pharmaceuticals, hopes to soon make ISS a new indication for the medication. In the meantime, it's being prescribed off-label for Donovan's condition."

"Is off-label prescribing safe?" Nancy wondered.

"Oh, yes. It happens all the time. It's virtually required in order to get around all the red tape of government regulations." Doctor Wilde chuckled, then reached into the bottom drawer of his desk and pulled out some brochures. "Take these home and talk it over. Give me a call if you have any questions. You'll want to make a decision fairly soon though. Donovan's almost sixteen. That gives us about a three-year window of opportunity for the drug to do its work."

Donovan didn't say much during the appointment. For the most part, he just sat in his chair, thunderstruck. The mere thought that his physical problems could be eliminated—or at least alleviated—was ecstatic.

After a bit, the Marsdens said their goodbyes and reassured the doctor that they'd be in touch. It wouldn't take long.

Alec Wilde sat behind his mahogany desk and pondered the situation. He had been monitoring Donovan's physical progress, or lack thereof, since becoming his physician two years ago. He knew the youngster to be an exceptionally kind, sweet, and intelligent boy. He also suspected that Donovan experienced far more than his share of teasing and bullying. But whenever he'd brought the subject up, Donovan had shied away from it. Alec knew that, in addition to having an exceedingly pleasing personality, his patient was equal parts introverted, insecure, and afraid. *Maybe Restor can change that,* he thought.

Pharmaceutical sales reps can be annoyingly slick, and the one from Braxton-Wentworth—Alec forgot his name—was no different. The lunchtime presentation was fully catered for the office staff, courtesy of the company: pizza, salad, chicken wings, bread sticks, and those yummy frosted cinnamon bites. He knew the sales rep was walking a fine line between FDA rules against marketing off-label drug use and First Amendment freedom of speech. But Alec didn't care.

He'd had Donovan in mind as the rep had cited the research and results related to Restor. Incredible outcomes with no noticeable side effects. Almost too good to be true.

Alec grabbed a Pepsi from the minifridge next to the desk and glanced at the calendar. Four years ago he had been a rising star at the Cleveland Clinic and an on-air CNN medical contributor. Now he was a general practitioner in Harbor Light. *My how times have changed.* Then his mind turned back to Donovan and Restor.

Almost too good to be true.

4

Diary entry of Donovan Marsden
dated April 1, 2018

I'm six foot one and buff and all the babes are into me. April Fools! Haha! I'd have to grow almost a foot in order for that to even begin to happen. The good news is I start the medication next month. Mom and Dad said it was okay. Dad pretty much insisted on it. Sometimes I think that my height bothers him more than it does me. I really do. I'll have to follow up with Dr. Wilde every couple of months to monitor how much I grow. I'm really excited about it! Even if I only grow a little bit, it'll have to be a whole lot better than it is now. Being small and ugly pretty much sucks. No girl is attracted to a scrawny runt with glasses, braces, and acne. I never had a girlfriend before. It would be really cool to have one. It really would. I could hold her hand and sing her songs. Pick flowers for her. Oh, keep dreaming Donovan. My birthday's coming up AND I'm finishing up my drivers ed. course. Dad said he might get me a car if I pass the test to get my license. Yay! That would be awesome to have my own car. I could drive out of town every day after school and just be by myself. Only a couple more months until summer break. I can't wait. I don't like school. I like the course work, but I don't like being around other kids. Maybe that will change after being on the medication for a while. :) Rodney says I better not get a big head if I get taller, haha. Ha! Butterscotch just jumped on the bed. He smells so good. I call him my aromatherapy kitty. Mikey and I like to play fetch with him with paper wads. It's so funny and cute. I love Butterscotch and I love Mikey. Well, I guess it's time to go to bed. Goodnight.

5

Harbor Light High had a strict policy that students' cell phones must be turned off during school hours, and no exceptions were made in Miss Chapman's algebra class. This forced Donovan and Rodney McAllister to engage in the antiquated art of note-passing. Since Donovan sat at the far back corner of the room, with Rodney situated to his immediate right, this was fairly easily accomplished. As Miss Chapman wrote an equation on the whiteboard (Judy Chapman eschewed modernities such as PowerPoint), a folded piece of notebook paper plopped on Donovan's desk.

Dude, Lisa Bailey's checkin' you out!

Lisa Bailey sat two seats over and one up from Rodney. A cute girl with light brown hair that was almost always pulled back in a ponytail, Lisa had never really registered in Donovan's mind, and he certainly didn't think that he'd ever registered in hers.

You must be imagining things he wrote back to Rodney.

No really! She keeps looking over at you and smiling. Looks like an opportunity has finally presented itself for you, loverboy, lol.

Lisa Bailey, Donovan thought. *Really? Would she really be interested in* me? And with that, the final bell of the day rang.

"Exercise four is your assignment for Monday," Miss Chapman said as the class bustled. "Have a nice weekend."

"See ya, Donovan," Rodney said, then scurried away to catch the bus.

"See ya."

Donovan stood up and slowly gathered his things together. Out of the corner of his eye he could see Lisa coming closer as she filed in line to leave the room. *Should I look at her as she walks by? Should I not even acknowledge her? What if she notices me looking at her, but she doesn't look back at me?*

And then it happened. Just before Lisa passed in front of him, Donovan looked up from his desk and their eyes met. She gave him an affectionate, toothy smile. He instinctively returned the gesture and instantly felt an immense warmth erupt in his gut. It was a good thing she didn't say anything to him, because he wouldn't have been able to respond due to the frog that jumped in his throat. Lisa walked by and he continued packing up his supplies. At that moment, the world, according to Donovan Marsden, was just.

6

The lasagna that had been enjoyed for lunch that day had been rearing its ugly head for hours, so Donovan finally found relief in the restroom after class. Now he was at his locker, packing his bookbag, and seemed to be the only one left in the school. He removed the Super High Bouncy Ball that he kept in his pocket for such occasions, and started down the hallway. He whipped the ball to the ground with his right hand. It bounced up, hit the far wall, and he caught it with the same hand.

Lisa Bailey. Yeah. Lisa, AND the medication he'll soon be taking, AND the car his dad would soon give him. Could it be that his life was taking a turn for the better? Could it be that spring had sprung in more ways than one? Donovan skipped down the spiral staircase to the first floor. He certainly had a spring in his step. He threw the ball a good forty feet at the wall, it bounced back, and he caught it perfectly. He hung a sharp left where the ball had previously hit and started traversing a dark corridor towards the exit. The overhead lights were burned out, and Donovan could only see the outside light at the exit door about fifty feet away. *Let's see if I can catch this one.* With a jump step, he hurled the ball down…and regretted it before it even hit the floor.

"Ow! Goddamnit, you little fuck!"

"Oh shoot! Sorry, Farrah."

7

Most high schools have somewhat of a caste system: jocks at the top; nerds at the bottom; others at various points in between. Harbor Light High, Home of the Mighty Panthers, was no different. Chad Chandler (the most popular guy in school) and Rodney McAllister were at polar ends of the spectrum. Donovan was certainly aware of his lowly existence with Rodney along the social totem pole. Farrah LaCroix, however, was an oddity.

John LaCroix, proprietor of LaCroix Financial Services, and his wife had divorced when Farrah was barely ten. After only a year of shared parenting, Farrah's mom had signed over full custodianship to John and left town. No one knew for sure why Beth LaCroix had loaded up her car and taken off for Cincinnati, sans the youngster. Not really. But there was a lot of speculation. The stylists at Beach Beauty Salon seemed to be hip to the latest gossip concerning practically everyone in town. One of them, Mary Zimmerman, had heard several stories about young Farrah. Like how she would throw ear-splitting tantrums in public if her mother didn't give her what she wanted. (John didn't have that problem; he always gave Farrah what she wanted.) Mary noticed that Beth had always looked tired, haggard, when it was her turn to have her daughter. In order to placate her, Beth had given Farrah a puppy for her eleventh birthday. Rumor had it that Farrah had killed the dog; accidentally or otherwise.

Since Farrah had no friends (nor seemed to want any), Beth had bought the golden retriever pup, and named her Millie, hoping that some sort of affection would grow in her little girl. Farrah had just ignored Millie, as loveable and adorable as she was. One night, after Beth had gone to bed, Farrah had sneaked into the living room and watched *The Exorcist* on HBO. Whereas virtually every other small child would be horrified by the movie, Farrah had been thoroughly entertained. In fact, she was curious. Could a human, or any animal for that matter, continue to live if you rotated its head all the way around? Just then, Millie wandered into the room, albeit reluctantly, and gave a low whimper. Farrah turned and looked at the dog…with a gleam in her eye.

As puppies do, Millie wanted to love and be loved by both humans in the household. Beth showered her with copious amounts of affection. But Millie didn't trust Farrah. Something about her scared her.

"Come here, Millie," Farrah whispered, patting the floor with her hand. "Come here, sweetie pie." Millie, head down to the carpet, slowly made her way toward Farrah. She stopped directly in front of her and whimpered again. Farrah gently stroked her back and scratched her head. It felt good to the puppy. She relaxed, lied down, and tilted her head back so she could enjoy the fingernails more. Maybe she could trust this human after all. Suddenly, Farrah pinned Millie to the floor with her left hand and clamped her muzzle shut with her extended right. She thought if she could gouge her thumb and middle finger into the dog's jaws, it would keep her from barking. She was right. She put all her weight on Millie's belly and began flexing her right wrist, thereby turning the pup's head to the right. Millie shivered all over and furiously scraped at the carpet with her hind legs as her head was being cranked. Crackling sounds, like those made from trampled-on sticks, emanated from just below her head, which was now turned almost one-hundred eighty degrees. Her tongue was sticking out, and her eyes bulged out of her head. Farrah kept cranking. Millie hissed. She peed on the carpet. At last, there came a *crick* sound, like a twig being snapped in half. Millie went limp. Farrah let go. No. I guess animals can't survive with their heads turned all the way around, she thought. Not dogs anyway.

Beth found Millie with her grotesquely tilted head in the living room the next morning. Farrah claimed she had accidently stepped on Millie, and that was what had caused her broken neck. It wasn't long after that that Beth began to believe her daughter was hopelessly wicked and wanted nothing more to do with her. John, who absolutely adored Farrah (even though the feeling wasn't mutual), gladly accepted total custody of his girl and didn't even want child support from Beth.

No, Farrah didn't have any true friends. Most girls, if they weren't intimidated by her, wanted to be her. Most guys, if they weren't intimidated by her, wanted to be with her. What Farrah lacked in terms of companionship, she more than made up for in money and breathtaking looks. With natural, almost platinum, blond hair that came down to mid-back and a tight, curvaceous body that was impossible not to notice, Farrah was the envy of the ladies. She headed the cheerleading squad (unusual for a junior, but the athletic boosters' generous donations from John LaCroix depended on it) only so that she could stay in shape and boss people around. It had nothing to do with school spirit, a concept she detested. Farrah was beautiful and she knew it. And tried immensely to maintain it. That was why she was more than a bit miffed when Donovan Marsden's Super High Bouncy Ball ricocheted off the floor.

And smacked her right in the eye.

8

Farrah and Chucky Vasquez (her current "boy-friend") happened to turn the corner when she caught the ball on her right eyebrow. Donovan didn't know Farrah—had never spoken with her—but, of course, he knew *of* her.

"You little runt bastard," she seethed. "This is the most unlucky day of your life!"

"Y-y-yeah, mostunluckydayofyourgoddamnlife," Chucky followed up. Chucky's speech impediment was such that it was often difficult for him to initiate a sentence. But once he got going, he would be on a roll. Farrah kept him around because he did what she said and he was fairly good in bed. She appreciated sexual aggressiveness and kinkiness. In fact, she demanded it. (That lame excuse for a man, Jimmy Parker, wouldn't even fuck her in the ass.)

Farrah grabbed Donovan's left bicep. "We're gonna teach you a lesson." She pushed him into the general supply room next to them and flipped on the light. She then shut the door. Locked it.

"Farrah, I'm so sorry. I didn't see—" She slapped him hard on the left side of his head and Donovan's glasses flew across the room. *Great,* he thought.

Another broken pair I'll have to explain to Mom and Dad.

"Chucky," Farrah said, "how should we punish this little turd?"

Chucky Vasquez, donned in his usual plain black T-shirt and saggy black jeans, rolled his eyes up and to the left with a look of dumb contemplation. His long, greasy black hair hung askew over his eyes. Being equal parts mean and moron made Chucky a dangerous character indeed. "H-h-howboutawedgie?"

"A wedgie. Yeah. But not *just* a wedgie. Make it hurt. Make it *really* hurt."

"Please," Donovan pleaded. "I didn't mean to—"

"Shut up and turn around!" Farrah barked.

Donovan, resigning himself to defeat, slowly turned around. He just hoped that it would be over soon with as little pain as possible.

Chucky grabbed Donovan's white Fruit of the Loom briefs with his right hand and yanked skyward, hard. Donovan felt an immediate searing sensation in the crack of his butt. "L-L-Likethatdontchabitch?" Chucky then added his left hand to the endeavor as if he was attempting a barbell curl, practically lifting his victim off the ground.

"Owwww!" Donovan had a horrific grimace painted on his tortured face as tears fell from both squinted eyes. He then felt and heard a rip as his briefs finally gave in.

"T-t-turnaroundyoutwerp."

As Donovan moved to face his tormentor, Chucky shot a quick blow with his fist just below the sternum, and Donovan crumpled to the floor in the fetal position. As icing on the cake, Chucky coughed up a wad of sputum and spat it on the back of Donovan's head.

"Don't even think about telling anyone about this," Farrah said. "And your punishments aren't over. Not by a longshot. Just how severe they'll be will depend on how black and blue my eye gets. Let's go, Chucky." As they were leaving, Farrah stopped and looked back. "Look at it this way. We did you a favor. You won't have to wipe your ass for a year." Chucky and Farrah laughed and walked out of the room.

Three minutes elapsed before Donovan could pick himself up off the floor and retrieve his glasses (which thankfully were intact) and backpack. He carefully and slowly made his way towards the exit, then remembered something. He went back down the hall and picked up his bouncy ball. *School lets out next month,* he thought. *And it can't come soon enough.* With that, Donovan placed his ball in his pocket and embarked on the slow journey home.

9

At the same time Donovan was making his moderately painful walk from school, Emily Wilde was tidying up in room 202. Tidying up after an extramarital romp had become commonplace for Emily over the past year or so. This afternoon's excursion had taken place at the Green Springs Motel in Norwalk, fifteen miles south of Harbor Light, with her flavor of the month; Tim the plumber.

The lead-up and the act itself were exciting, but she always had the same feelings afterward. Emptiness. Regret. *Why do you do it?* she had asked herself several times, almost daily. She didn't know why. She would have never cheated on Alec in the past; in the life they'd had before...before their perfect world had come crumbling down. She guessed that her trysts were her way of escaping, albeit temporarily, the depressing existence she now had. Life (and Alec) had indeed changed. Changed for the worse.

"Um," Tim muttered as he walked out of the bathroom with his work gear back on. "I guess I'll...see you around."

"Yeah. Sure. Text me."

Tim gave her a half-smile, looked down, and exited the room.

With a guilt-laden ache creeping in her gut, Emily gathered her belongings and stuffed them in her purse. She didn't notice the tear that streamed down her left cheek.

10

That evening while nursing his sore bum, Donovan texted on his Samsung with his best friend—his only friend—Rodney:

Dude, you have to tell someone
about this!

> No Rodney I just want to let it
> go. I don't want to stir up any
> more trouble.

Well, just stay out of their way I
guess. Summer's almost here
and you won't have to worry
about it anymore.

> Yeah that's what I was thinking.
> But I can't stay out of people's
> way any more than I have. I'm
> not the Invisible Man, lol.

LMAO! I guess not. So what do
you think about Lisa Bailey,
loverboy?

I've been thinking about her all
afternoon. It's weird. On the
same day I get the worst wedgie
of my life, my mind is on her,
lol.

Consider it therapy, dude. I def.
think she's into you. You should
talk to her. Anyway, my old
man's barking about something.
Until next time loverboy. Later.

Later.

11

"Mellinger! Artie Mellinger! Gitcher ass in here, boy."

"General—"

"We can dispense with the formalities, Artie. Have a seat. There are reasons why I wanted to talk with you directly, instead of going through the regular channels. I want to make sure we're crystal clear. This is likely the last time we'll ever discuss Spharion A. I don't care to hear or say the term 'Spharion A' ever again after today. Want some coffee?"

"No, thank you, sir."

"Mellinger, what the hell's an egghead like you doing over here anyway? Shouldn't you be burning through the dean's list at some Ivy League school? And don't give me that 'to serve my country' horseshit."

"Well, sir. As an *egghead*, I guess I wanted to get out of my shell and see the world. Do some good. On the government's dime."

"And here we are in the world's armpit. Okay. Down to business. Spharion A. The original chemical compound of Agent Yellow. Goddamn rainbow herbicides. Oh, just so you know, although Spharion B is apparently safer, we'll likely do away with Agent Yellow altogether in the next few months. Too many...uh...complications. Artie, in your final report, you wrote that it's 'almost certain' that Spharion A is responsible for the...uh...atrocities. I want you to change terms such as 'almost certain' and 'likely' with terms like 'maybe' and 'possibly' and 'unknown'."

"But, sir, the evidence, as you know, is virtually absolute—"

"Goddamn it, Artie! I don't want to hear that bullshit! I want to put this damn thing to rest. Otherwise it could haunt us for decades. Now...I'm not asking you to lie and rewrite the whole thing. It would just be...appreciated...if you would switch words like 'probable' with words like 'possible.' Understood?"

"Yes, sir."

"I want the revised report on my desk today, no later than 1700. Now, how're the folks?"

12

"**P**ass the salt," Rodney said, "and the pepper. This needs a little spicing up." Donovan and Rodney were munching during freshman lunch period, where they solely occupied the same circular table all year. Today's menu was rather appetizing too: Salisbury steak, mashed potatoes, peas, a peanut butter cookie, and orange drink. "Thanks. Whatcha gettin for your birthday?"

"I don't know," Donovan replied, "but I hope it's a car. You *know* that. I don't even care what model it is, just so I can—"

"Hey, loverboy, Lisa Bailey's lookin over here!" Brief pause. "She's comin over!"

Donovan turned around just as Lisa was approaching the table. She stood next to him sporting a blue blazer and khaki slacks and the ever-present ponytail. "Hey, guys," Lisa said shyly. "May I join you?"

"Why soitanly," Rodney responded in his best Curly Howard impression.

She sat at Donovan's immediate left. "Hi, Donovan."

"Hi, Lisa."

They exchanged a quick glance, then dropped their eyes down to their lunch trays. A moment of awkwardness followed that was mercifully broken by Rodney. "Hey, Lisa. Today is Donovan's birthday. Sweet sixteen! Yeah, baby!"

"Oh, wow! Happy birthday, Donovan." Then, she wanted to put her foot in her mouth as soon as she followed up with, "Isn't sixteen a little old for a freshman?"

"Yeah," Donovan responded. "My parents held me back, hoping I'd blend in more with the other kids size-wise."

"Oh," she said. The awkwardness resumed. "I'm going back for more napkins. You guys need anything?"

"Perhaps a time machine set to summer break. Nyuck-nyuck-nyuck," Rodney joked, and both Lisa and Donovan chuckled. As soon as Lisa got up and left the table, Rodney began stuffing his face with the remnants on his tray.

"What are you doing?" Donovan asked, bewildered.

"Mmm...dude..." Rodney swallowed hard. "It's time for you to make a move. Knock her socks off. You got this, loverboy."

"But—"

Rodney picked up his tray and headed for the exit, leaving Donovan, momentarily, alone. His hands shook and a flush of red ran up his cheeks. *What should I say when she gets back?* he wondered. *Should I be flirty? Maybe ask her on a date? Jeez, I don't even know what a date is. Maybe I'll act like I'm not interested. Oh, Donovan, just be your—*

"Here you go," Lisa said as she resumed her seat. "Happy birthday. Sorry, but it was the best I could do on the spur of the moment." She placed in front of Donovan's tray another cookie and an origami flower constructed from a napkin. "Do you like it?"

"Oh, wow! I love it!"

"It's a lotus. Origami is kind of a hobby of mine."

"Thank you, Lisa. It's beautiful."

"You're welcome. Had I known before, I would've given you a much better present."

Lisa and Donovan spent the next few minutes finishing their meals in silence—and smiling at each other. At last she broke the quiet: "Well, I guess I better get to my next class. Talk to you soon?"

"Yeah," he replied. "I'm looking forward to it." He noticed Lisa leaving the table with a wide grin on her face.

Donovan spent the next minute or so taking it all in. He supposed that for the remainder of the school day, Lisa would be on his mind just as much as the prospect of getting a car for his birthday. He couldn't stop smiling. *This is turning out to be a great day, for sure.*

Yeah, baby.

13

After dinner, Nancy brought out the cake (Bugs Bunny holding a basketball) and led the Marsden family rendition of "Happy Birthday." Even Butterscotch was in the kitchen/dining room to celebrate. Donovan was starting to think he wouldn't be getting a car after all.

"Okay, sweetie," Nancy said after lighting all sixteen candles, "make a wish."

Can I make two? To be taller AND win Lisa Bailey's heart?

Donovan blew out the candles and the family clapped. (Even Joe, who was normally subdued, cheered.)

"What'dya ask for, Donovan?" Mikey asked eagerly.

"I can't tell you, Mikey, or else it won't come true."

"Before we dig in," Joe said as he set down his beer, "let's go outside, buddy. I want to show you something."

Donovan assumed he was about to be scolded for leaving something in the yard as his father and he walked out the back door. But, when they turned toward the rear of the shed, he suddenly stopped in his tracks, stunned. There it was: a white sedan.

"2009 Ford Fusion," Joe said. "I got a good deal on it from a friend. Well, what do ya think?"

"It's beautiful," was all Donovan could manage.

"Yeah, I think so too," Joe replied. "Let's go have some cake, then we'll take it for a spin."

As Mikey and Donovan were working on their second pieces of cake alone, Joe came back into the room with a wrapped gift. "I almost forgot. I picked this up yesterday, but your mom and I wanted to wait to give it to you today. Go ahead and open it."

The brothers exchanged a glance, and the younger sibling just shrugged. Donovan tore off the packaging with just two pulls, and received yet another shock of the day. In his hands were two thirty-day-supply boxes of Restor. He looked up at his father with a toothy grin.

"I pray that stuff works," Joe said.

"Me, too," Donovan replied.

14

Donovan was winding down his euphoric day, in the bathroom, with his Restor kit. He gazed at himself in the mirror—completely nude with the exception of his glasses—and wondered just how effective this drug could be. He hated his appearance, hated looking at himself, especially when naked, but he forced a hard analysis: mid-length brownish-blond hair (almost the same color as Lisa's); black-rimmed glasses; acne; scrawny arms and legs; non-existent pectorals; pasty white skin. The only part of himself that he liked was his mouthwash-blue eyes, but they were hard to notice behind his dorky glasses. He used a measuring tape to assess his height. An even five feet. He then opened the package of Restor and remembered his consultation with Dr. Wilde the previous week:

Donovan, you'll be given a two-month supply, at the end of which you'll need to see me for a follow-up. If all is going well, I'll renew your prescription for another couple of months. We'll just go along with that schedule and play it by ear. As long as you're responding to the medication and don't have any bad reactions to it, you'll likely be on it for about three years. Don't expect results right away. In fact, you may not notice any change at all during your first two-month cycle. Okay? Any questions or concerns? I hope this drug makes all your dreams come true.

Donovan removed a plastic tray from the box. It consisted of thirty depressions, each filled with a needle and cartridge. He unscrewed the cap of the instrument's chamber and dropped in a cartridge. After replacing the cap, he attached the short needle at the other end. The entire "pen" was about six inches long.

You can make the injection anywhere between the lower rib cage and the top of your pelvis. Just stay at least two inches away from the belly button. And don't inject into the same location every time. Move it around.

Donovan decided that tonight's injection, the very first, would be made slightly above the navel, about three inches to the left. He held the pen in his right fist, positioned it downward at a forty-five-degree angle, per Dr. Wilde's instructions, and inserted the needle into his belly. The pain, which Donovan had thought would be excruciating, turned out to be very tolerable. Just a pinch. He then used his right thumb to depress the cap, pushing the medicine into his body. After that, he disassembled the needle and cartridge and disposed of them in a special container that came with the kit. And that was that. Donovan again looked at himself in the mirror...and smiled.

I hope this drug makes all your dreams come true.

"Me, too."

15

While Donovan was giving himself the first of his daily injections, Alec and Emily Wilde were finishing up a late meal at home. Tonight's cuisine: Chinese take-out served on generic dinnerware. Gone was the fine china they used to dine with. That, as well as other luxury items, had been auctioned off.

They lived on Butte Street, not far from her general law practice, in a neighborhood that most would agree was fairly well-to-do for Harbor Light. It was a far cry from their beachfront condo in Lakewood (where many young up-and-comers reside), but it sufficed. At least it sufficed for Alec.

"It's supposed to rain tomorrow," Emily said after a long period of silence. "Don't forget your umbrella."

She was drinking pinot. He was drinking Pepsi.

"Em—"

"Alec, don't."

"Look, I know I've said 'I'm sorry' a lot about this—"

Emily started to say that *she* was sorry; to make a full confession of her infidelities. Then, she changed her mind and closed her mouth.

"I know this isn't what you're used to," Alec said, and dropped his head.

"It's not what either of us are used to," she replied. "It's okay, though. It'll just take a little more time to—adjust."

Emily got up from the table to refill her glass. That she had plenty of time to adjust was a fucking understatement. After two years in Harbor Light, however, the adjustment just wasn't happening.

Alec Wilde and Emily Nordstrom had met in 1991, on a blind date arranged by mutual friends. He was midway through his medical studies at Case Western Reserve. She was a second-year law student at Cleveland-Marshall. She didn't remember when she had fallen in love with him. It could have started on that first date at Broadview Lanes. Alec would purposely throw gutter balls and make wisecracks about it. Emily laughed almost nonstop. He wasn't like the guys she was used to dating, and she found that refreshing.

Emily was raised in a proper upper-middle-class household in a suburb of Dayton. The boyfriends that her parents tried to arrange for her were, well, boring. Alec was different. *Much* different. To start, he was from the other side of the tracks. He was considered a non-traditional student in that he hadn't started college right after high school. No one in his family had ever gone to college. So Alec worked as a laborer in-small town Ohio for five years, give or take, before finding his muse. Emily quickly discovered that he was goofy, witty, funny, and, most of all, not like other guys. His hair was dark brown with a touch of gray, and it fell to just below the shoulders; not at all like the plastered buzz cuts of those who had previously courted her. He was also original.

"Close your eyes," Alec had said while they took a break from tossing bowling balls to enjoy some pizza. "And hold out your hand."

"Okay," Emily said with a chuckle. She felt a small, light object placed in her palm.

"Open."

Emily opened her eyes and was a bit befuddled to be looking at a green stone.

"It's jade. I found it years ago while working in a quarry. I figured that if this date went well, then I'd give this to you as an expression of my interest to see you again."

"It's so pretty," Emily said, smiling. "And yes, I'd like to see you again, too."

And she meant it. In spite of, or perhaps in addition to, his apparent penchant for beer drinking (Alec polished off two pitchers himself at the alley), she was blown away by this guy. They moved in together within three months.

Emily filled her glass halfway and finished the wine with two gulps. She placed the glass in the sink and came back into the dining room.

"I'm going to bed," she said. "Coming?"

"Nah. I'm gonna stay up and catch the news."

Emily took that as code that he'd be spending another night sleeping on the recliner. Such was their life now.

16

At last, the final day of school had arrived, and Donovan was more than a little relieved. But a part of him was also a bit melancholy. He thought of Lisa as he drove to school in his new used Fusion. *Will I see her this summer?* They made quite a bit of small talk and had been more than a tad bit flirtatious over the last couple of weeks. He was certain she would agree to a date if he asked. *What would we do?* More importantly, *How would I pay for it?* He would have to get a job during summer break, but in the meantime he was sure his dad would lend him the money. Heck, his dad would probably be so excited that his son had started dating, he'd *give* him the money. Maybe dinner and a movie. That seemed to be the old standby. He decided that he would ask her out after today's algebra class.

During first-period gym, Donovan was dressed in his usual uniform (a plain white T-shirt and beige shorts more suitable for lounging than exercise). The kids had running drills, then finished with a game of dodgeball. (Donovan, not surprisingly, was one of the first to get tagged out.)

Most likely due to a combination of teenage modesty and lack of time (Mr. Barrison often conducted class right up until the bell rang), the boys would typically skip showering after gym. At best, they may have washed off with water at a sink (what Rodney called a whore bath) before putting back on their regular clothes. But today was a little different for Donovan. He had worked up a good sweat this morning. Today he would ask Lisa out on a date, and he didn't want to smell ripe while doing it. He figured he would have about ten minutes (plenty of time) to shower before the bell sounded for next period. On his way to the boys' locker room, out of the corner of his eye, he saw Farrah, Chucky, and Ted Mullins strolling through the empty cafeteria, which was adjacent to the gym. *Ted Mullins? Wasn't he expelled last year?* The thought quickly left him.

Donovan's shower lasted a little longer than he had projected. The steaming hot water felt so good on his face. And Donovan felt good too. Wonderful. It was the last day of school and he was hoping—planning—to have an awesome summer.

Seth Peters and Curt Yaklovich were the only ones remaining in the locker area, which was located next to the shower stalls. They were making small talk as they gathered their belongings in their gym bags.

Seth: "How was Prom? Get laid?"

Curt: "It was a'right. Nah. She just let me get to second base. Whatcha up to this summer?"

They didn't see Chucky Vasquez creeping up behind them.

"G-g-getlost!"

They got lost.

Donovan turned the water off and dried himself with one of the standard-issue starched white towels that were available for the students to use. He looked down as he fumbled with the towel, which was gathered just below his chest. He noticed how cold the air and floor got as he strode out of the stall and passed the toilets. When he got to the locker area, he stopped. Looked up with his nearsighted eyes. And gasped.

17

Ted Mullins rounded out Farrah LaCroix's inner circle of ne'er-do-wells. He sported a mildly handsome retro look with his shoulder-length sandy brown hair, parted in the middle and feathered. Although not quite as bright as Farrah, he could have amounted to something had he not gone the other way and majored in the fine art of douchebaggery.

Last year, Mr. Harris, the business teacher, had caught Ted smoking a joint on school grounds. Mr. Harris had responded by stating that he was reporting Ted to the principal. Ted had responded by threatening to break Mr. Harris's legs. Ted's laundry list of school infractions was quite impressively long, and this was Principal Winter's opportunity to be rid of him for good. In a closed-door session, Mr. Harris had agreed not to press charges, and Ted's barely-coherent, opioid-addicted mom had agreed that Ted would technically "drop out." An expulsion wouldn't be on his record.

"Y'know, you sure are a little shit," Ted said. Donovan just stood there at the bathroom entrance to the locker room, frozen with fear.

"Yeah, and you're not so tough without your ball, are you?" Farrah followed. "Speaking of balls, let's see what you're hiding under there, big fella." Farrah (who had no qualms about being in a boys' locker room) slithered over to Donovan and, before he had time to react, tore his towel off of him. "Haaaaa!" she shrieked.

The three-to-one parts mixture of fear and after-shower cold air had pulled Donovan's testicles way up into his belly, and had shriveled his penis to practically nothing. Tiny genitalia on a tiny body.

"Honey, you're obviously a virgin," Farrah said smiling, "but when the time comes to lose it, do you think any girl will be satisfied with that little thing?"

"Y-y-yougottalittlefuckinpeterman."

"Y'know, I almost feel sorry for ya," Ted smirked at Donovan. "Almost."

"Please. Please just leave me alone," was all that Donovan, now clutching his privates, could barely get out. He thought about screaming at the top of his lungs in order to attract attention and be rescued. He once heard that if you needed assistance, the right word to yell is *Fire!*, not *Help!* Apparently, people are far more interested in observing something macabre, than to get out of their comfort zone and help someone. *It's none of my business* seems to be the general consensus. Even so, screaming for help, though it might save his skin at the moment, might actually serve to make the situation worse in the long run. Farrah's "punishments"—that was the word she used—might get prolonged, and the severity, much worse. No. Donovan wouldn't yell for help. He'd bear this and hope to come out relatively unscathed.

"Even though you just showered, I don't think you were very thorough. I think I see a smudge behind your ear," Farrah said. "We can fix that."

"What do you have in mind?" Ted asked.

"Last time it was a wedgie. Now I think it's time for a swirlie," she said.

"Oh, God, no," Donovan muttered.

Farrah turned her head to Chucky and said, "Why don't you warm up the shitter?" Chucky responded with a stupid grin, baring teeth that would have made every dentist in Harbor Light cringe. He went to the nearest commode to do his business.

"Please, Farrah. I don't have anything against you. And I'm sorry about—"

"You're sorry, alright," she interrupted. "A sorry little pussy."

"Why are you doing this to me?"

Farrah leaned over him with a deep scowl on her face, lips pressed into a tight white line. "Because. I. Can." She stared at him for several seconds. Donovan kept his eyes to the floor. "Jesus fucking christ, Chucky! Are you done?"

A moment later, when Chucky finished urinating (which seemed to Donovan to take forever), he called out, "A-alldone!"

Without speaking, Farrah and Ted each took Donovan under an arm and escorted him to the front of the toilet. He looked into the bowl at a mixture that was a deep yellow, almost orange. His stomach clenched. They then forced him onto his knees.

Donovan whimpered.

"Y'know, you might wanna hold your breath," Ted said, right before plunging Donovan's head into the bowl.

Perhaps if Donovan had been calm, cool, and collected, he could have held his breath and ridden the whole thing out until the tormentors stopped (either voluntarily, or by way of someone walking into the locker room).

But that wasn't the case.

He was excited. Nervous. Afraid. Within ten seconds of having his head submerged in the tepid water/piss solution, Donovan coughed; then inhaled; then puked.

Ted pulled Donovan up. "Y'know, you sure are making a mess."

Farrah: "Do it again."

"Down ya go, shithead." Ted pushed him down again, only this time Donovan resisted. He placed his hands on the toilet's rim trying to keep from going down. To no avail. Ted smacked his right arm away and muscled his head back into the bowl, smacking it on the bottom of the porcelain. Now a tinge of red was blending with the yellow-orange.

Donovan lost control of his bladder and peed down his left thigh.

"Hahaha! You're now covered with piss, you little fuck," Farrah said.

Donovan took another gulp and reflexively vomited it back out. His arms and legs were flailing. He thought, *I'm going to pass out.*

"WHAT THE HELL IS GOING ON!"

18

Growing up in the Brightmoor neighborhood of Detroit in the 1980s was certainly no treat. Brightmoor (what many called "Blight More") had been going downhill for some time. The city as a whole never really recovered from the 1967 Twelfth Street Riot, a five-day horror that claimed forty-three lives. And since the '50s, auto and other manufacturing jobs had steadily left the city. As the jobs moved out, poverty (and poverty's first cousin, crime) moved in. And the various criminal activities seemed to become more organized; organized by a group called the D Street Kings, a local affiliate of a little-known, yet growing, nationwide gang known as the Crips.

It was in the summer of 1985 when ten-year-olds Charles "Mooky" DeValle and Jermaine Barrison met (and immediately befriended) on one of Brightmoor's many outdoor basketball courts. (Mooky had earned his moniker a little earlier that year on the court. One of the older kids had noticed Charles's zeal while at play, and yelled, "Look at dat boy runnin all 'round, lookin likea monkey!" *Monkey* was soon shortened to *Mooky*, and the nickname stuck.) Both boys were recently new to the area, emigrating from downtown. They took to each other instantly, and shared a love of basketball, Atari, comic books, candy, and bubble gum. Girls were not yet on the radar.

Mook and Maine.

Maine and Mook.

Two peas in a pod. They went together like Mike and Ike.

The boys had something else in common.

There exists a subtle, often-times unspoken, rift within the African-American community between those who are considered *light-skinned*, and those considered *dark-skinned*. Jermaine and Mooky were of the latter category. In Euro-centric America, even among fellow blacks, darker-shaded folks can feel alienated, as if others look down their noses at them. Just another bond the two shared.

They only got in trouble once. It happened a year after they became besties. Brightmoor Meats was a favorite of the boys for snacks and comics. One August day, on a double-dare, they decided to smuggle one pouch each of grape-flavored Big League Chew bubble gum (their favorite) in their shorts. They didn't even make it to the front door.

Mister Stigliano, the owner of the butcher shop, was more hurt than angry. He knew these were good boys, and they had been frequenting his store for months. "I don't need to tell yoos that it's wrong to steal, do I?" he said. The boys looked first at each other, then at the floor, teary-eyed. "Tell ya what. Police don't need to know 'bout dis. Parents don't need to know. You two yutes stop in ev'ry so often. Help me put stuff away. Clean the place up a little. I'll tro in all the comics yoos can read and a few bucks on toppa dat. Deal?" Mooky and Jermaine worked part-time at Brightmoor Meats for the next four years.

The two entered Redford High School (which boasted George C. Scott as an alumnus) in the fall of '89. Differences—physical and emotional—became apparent between them. Jermaine was sprouting up, tall and well-developed for his age. He also had a firm resolve and was able to simply ignore some of the rather nefarious aspects of his environment. Mooky, on the other hand, was another story. He was having a rougher go at life. Mook was smaller-than-average. Among his other attributes: having a proverbial heart of gold; demure; eager to please; easily influenced. A bad combination for a boy trying to survive in the hood.

Run by a twenty-three-year-old shark simply known as Lincoln, the D Street Kings had tightened its influence on the community. Lincoln wanted to climb the Crips' ladder by using the Kings as a vehicle. Realizing that there is power in numbers, he wanted to inflate his group's membership, thereby crowding out rival gangs and increasing his own prominence. He would target young boys who seemed vulnerable by using a soft-sell courting technique. He would seemingly befriend them by introducing himself as a community leader who sincerely cared about the kids and the neighborhood. He'd tell them that they could have a much higher social status if they aligned with the Kings and did minor *jobs* for him. He'd also pay them with money and candy. These *jobs* typically entailed running drugs and guns as middle-men.

It was on a cloudy Saturday in April of 1990, during their lunch break at an Evergreen Road Wendy's, when Mooky Devalle told Jermaine Barrison about his chance-encounter with Lincoln.

"Aww, Mooky, no."

"'Maine, you don't understand. All I'd have to do is deliver packages."

"And do you know what's *in* those packages? Probably heroin, firearms, and God knows what else. Everything that makes this hood stink. Man, you're better than that."

"That's easy for you to say," a defensive Mooky said. "Ain't no one laughin at *you*. Ain't no one makin fun of *you*. I be nice to girls, and they come back by callin me *crispy* and all that. You're the same color as me. Ain't nobody call you *crispy*. You don't know what it's like to get picked on. Picked on to the point you can't take it no more."

Jermaine dropped his eyes to the table with an expression of solid disappointment.

"Look, Jermaine. I'm just gonna do a few jobs and see how it goes. I don't know what's in those packages, and I don't wanna know. Just a few jobs, that's all." Mooky looked to his best friend, hoping to receive, if not approval, anything other than outright revulsion.

Jermaine stood up, polished off his Frosty, and without even looking at Mooky said, "You're better than that," and walked off.

The boys' relationship was strained over the next couple weeks. They didn't communicate much at work or school. *I'll fix that tomorrow*, Jermaine thought as he watched an NBA game in his apartment one Friday night. They were both scheduled to work at Mr. S's store the following day. *I'll reach out to Mook. Let him know that even though I don't like what he's doin, he's still my best friend and I love 'im. Yeah. We'll patch it up.* He missed his friend, who was more like a brother. He would repair their kinship and it would be like before: Mook and Maine; Maine and Mook.

Except Jermaine didn't get the chance.

While Jermaine sat contemplating the rejuvenation of his relationship with Mooky, Mook was running a *job*. Special delivery for a destination on Dacosta Street (from which the D Street Kings had gotten their name). Someone named Quincy.

Before muttering the last sentence of his life, Mooky gently tapped on the door.

A man fitting Quincy's description opened it. Mooky walked into the foyer, handed over the parcel, then turned to leave.

"Waita minute!" the man who was presumably Quincy yelled. "Gotta check it out!"

Lincoln had heard rumors that Quincy, who was known to be high-strung and hot-tempered, was a spy for the Bloods, the Crips' main rival gang. He thought he would test Quincy by deliberately short-changing him, and judge his reaction.

Quincy removed a switchblade from his back left pocket and opened the parcel. He counted the money.

"What da fuck is this?" His massive globes of eyeballs raged at Mooky. "Where's da rest of it?"

"I'm just the messenger," was all that a scared-shitless Mooky could say.

"Fuckin lyin, cheatin Crip bastads!"

Quincy then removed a .45 semi-automatic from his waistband. And blew a hole through Mooky's chest.

Quincy disappeared, and Mooky's murder was never solved. The following year, Jermaine's stepdad got a new job and relocated the family to the sleepy community of Farmington Hills. Upon graduation (Jermaine was the first of his family to earn a high school diploma), Jermaine embarked on a new life by joining the Army. A few years into his service, he began taking courses toward a Master's in Education. He figured that he'd like to be a gym teacher when he got out of the military.

19

Farrah, Chucky, and Ted each took two steps back. Donovan collapsed on the tiled floor, coughing. Jermaine did a quick check on him, as the other three made moves toward the door.

"Stop right there!"

"Well, well. Mister Barrison saves the day," Farrah said truculently.

Jermaine knew enough about Farrah and her influence to know that she was the one to address. His six-foot-two frame got within inches of her face.

"Cupcake, I don't care who you are. And I don't care who your daddy is. One more stunt like that and you'll be expelled just like your little wretched buddy here."

Ted stepped up to Jermaine.

"Listen up, nigger," Ted said. "That's right. I don't go to school here no more. And I'm under eighteen. So y'know, that means you can't touch me."

Jermaine clenched his fists and tempered himself with a deep inhale. "If I ever see you on school grounds again, then I'll personally throw you out like the trash you are."

"Oh c'mon Mr. Barrisonnn," Farrah said as she teasingly swiveled her hips. "I thought all you darkies like blond white girls who are put together like this." She then pushed her blue skirt up to just below her buttocks, and winked.

"All three of you get out of my sight. Now!"

20

While Donovan took another shower, Jermaine informed Donovan's study hall monitor that he would be excused today. Jermaine had an open period, so they could talk. The two of them sat in Jermaine's small office, off to the side of the locker room, the teacher behind his basic, metallic desk, the student directly in front of him. Jermaine cleaned the cut on Donovan's head and put a Band-Aid on it.

"How are you feeling?" Jermaine said.

"Okay, I guess. Just a little sick in the stomach, that's all."

"Drink some more of that ginger ale. It'll help." Jermaine leaned forward and folded his hands together. "According to regulations, I should report this." Donovan dropped his eyes down. "But I have a feeling you don't want me to do that."

"It would only make it worse," Donovan muttered without looking up.

"I suppose it would. On the bright side, it's the last day of school and hopefully you won't see those punks all summer. By the time school starts again in the fall, they probably will have long forgotten about you." Jermaine said this last part without really believing it.

For the next twenty minutes, Jermaine asked Donovan about his *story*, and Donovan gave it. The taunts, the teasing, the physical bullying, his hopes for Restor—even Lisa Bailey. Not knowing why, he felt comfortable talking with Mr. Barrison.

And also not knowing why, Jermaine was fascinated with what Donovan had to say. He never took any personal interest in his students (thinking it was professionally safer just to show up and do his job), but he felt genuine concern for this tiny boy sitting in front of him. He didn't know why he felt such sympathy for Donovan,

Mooky.

but as the boy was talking about his medication for idiopathic short stature (which Jermaine figured wouldn't work at all; just another profit avenue of the almighty drug makers), an idea came to him.

"I'm the strength and conditioning coach for the football team," Jermaine said. "And I could uuuse…an assistant. Someone to help me set up before the players get here and start their weight-lifting sessions."

Donovan started to perk up.

"It would just be the two of us in the weight room," he continued. "And I could show you some basic exercises to put some bulk on you. And maybe I could show you some basic self-defense moves in case your…*friends*…ever mess with you again. I'm sure I could get the school board to make it a paid position. Sounds like you could use some money to woo this gal you're into. Whatd'ya think?"

Donovan was now grinning like a kid on Christmas morning.

"Gee, Mr. Barrison," he said, "that'd be awesome!"

"The sessions start next Monday at eleven. Why don't you meet me here at nine? Wear comfortable clothes, like your gym class attire."

"Thank you so much, Mr. Barrison. I'll be a really good assistant."

"I know you will."

They shook hands. The bell rang.

21

Donovan, understandably, felt ill and was allowed to go home and take his final exams the following week during teachers' conferences. He explained the cut on his head to his parents by saying that he had fallen during gym class.

He didn't do much that week. He hung out with Rodney and played with Mikey. What was on his mind the most was the opportunity to assist Mr. Barrison the following Monday. But he had something else on his mind as well.

The last time he had seen Lisa was before his little incident with Farrah et al. They'd kept in touch via texting, and Donovan wanted to ask her out soon. He thought of something that would be much better than dinner-and-a-movie for a first date: the Strawberry Fest.

Traditionally, Memorial Day marks the beginning of the summer season. However, many in Harbor Light celebrate the advent of summer with that year's Strawberry Fest, always held two weeks after Memorial Day weekend. That's where you can partake in all things strawberry: strawberry pie, strawberry shortcake, strawberry cupcakes, strawberry wine, strawberry jam, strawberry pop (in Ohio, soda is referred to as *pop*), strawberry gelatin—did I mention strawberries? Yeah, that would be the perfect event for Donovan and Lisa to get to know each other. Really get to know each other, not just texting or making small talk in the classroom or cafeteria.

After Sunday night's injection, he summoned the courage to call Lisa and ask her if she would accompany him to Strawberry Fest the following Saturday (she said yes!). He lied down on his bed with his hands folded behind his head and Butterscotch at his feet. He thought of Lisa and anticipated tomorrow's appointment with Mr. Barrison (who was by far the coolest teacher in school). He fell asleep grinning.

22

It was a clear, cloudless, sunny morning on June 4 when Donovan met Mr. Barrison at school. They did their work, which included setting out towels, bottles of water, weight lifting charts, and tidying up the exercise area. They finished up about an hour before the athletes were scheduled to arrive.

"Alright. Time to start your training. I'm going to show you some exercises that'll make you grow like a weed."

Grow like a weed, Donovan thought. *I like that.*

"I'm gonna give you a total-body workout that'll take about a half-hour to complete, three days per week. You can do all your training here, Mondays, Wednesdays, and Fridays. What do you think about that?"

Donovan didn't know what to think. "Gee, Mr. Barrison, I really appreciate you helping me." He thought for a second. "Should I call you Mr. Barrison or Coach Barrison?"

"Tell you what. Since we're gonna be seeing a lot of each other this summer, why don't you start calling me Jermaine?"

"Okay. Jermaine." Donovan beamed.

"You don't need to do a complete bodybuilding routine in order to develop an awesome physique," Jermaine explained. "What I'm about to show you is basically the same routine I've been doing for years." Donovan knew that the training program must work. Mr. Barrison, Jermaine, with his chiseled body, shaved bald head, and shortly-trimmed combination mustache-goatee, looked somewhere between Terry Crews and a young Louis Gossett Jr.

Jermaine led the boy through seven exercises (weights and calisthenics) that incorporated all of the major muscle groups: bicep curls, reverse bicep curls, wrist curls, reverse wrist curls, push-ups, calf raises, and free squats. He demonstrated to Donovan strict, proper form for each exercise. He showed him how to exhale during the contraction (the positive) and inhale during the relaxation (the negative) with each repetition. He instructed him to perform two sets of each upper-body exercise to failure (meaning that the last repetition couldn't be completed). The two lower-body exercises were to be performed for five minutes, each.

"The team will start coming in any time now," Jermaine said. "You're going to be sore for the rest of the week from today's workout. Instead of working out on Wednesday, I'll show you some martial arts moves. It's basically an eclectic style of jujitsu I put together during my time in the military."

Chad Chandler walked into the weight room. He looked at Jermaine: "Hey, Coach Barrison." He then looked at Donovan: "Hey."

"Hey," Donovan replied.

"See you Wednesday, young man," Jermaine winked.

"See ya Wednesday."

As Donovan walked out on rubbery legs, Jermaine wondered if he would indeed see him on Wednesday. He had his doubts.

23

Diary entry of Donovan Marsden
dated June 8, 2018

Mr. Barrison, I mean Jermaine, told me I'd be sore all week and he didn't lie. It's hard getting used to calling him by his first name. Instead of working out on Wednesday, he taught me some jujitsu moves upstairs on the mats that the wrestlers use. Jujitsu is mainly a grappling martial art. Jermaine said that my structure is so small I'd probably break my own hand if I punched someone in self-defense. I really would. So he's going to teach me a couple of grappling moves after the workouts. The school board was able to approve getting me paid on the three days a week I help set up for the football team's strength and conditioning sessions. It only amounts to three hours a week, and of course I don't get paid to exercise and practice jujitsu, haha. It's not much, but it's gas money. I'll have to find more of a full-time job if I want to have a decent summer. Rodney got a job at the library. Lucky guy. Oh, I'm so excited about tomorrow! I'm going to pick Lisa up at ten and then we'll get to spend the entire day at Strawberry Fest! I told Jermaine about it, and he said he was proud of me. He also gave me an advance on my paycheck, so I'll have some money to spend on Lisa tomorrow. I hope I make a great impression on her. Well, time to hit the sack. Goodnight.

24

Mike Bailey was less-than-thrilled when his fifteen-year-old daughter told him that a boy would be picking her up to *hang out*. Mike took that as teenspeak for a *date*. He envisioned some hulking lineman trying to have his way with Mike and Lola's little girl. But when he opened the front door at 547 Emerson Street in response to the knocking, he had to stifle a laugh.

"Hello, Mr. Bailey. I'm Donovan Marsden. Is Lisa here?"

Donovan, who appeared to Mike to be no older than twelve, extended his hand, and the formerly concerned father shook it. He then took a peek at the Fusion in the driveway and figured the boy couldn't be half-bad (Mike worked at the Ford assembly plant in Avon Lake). "Uh, yeah—"

"Hi, Donovan," Lisa said as she scampered to the door. "Bye, Dad. I'll be home this afternoon."

"Uh, bye." Mike watched for a moment as Donovan opened the passenger-side door for his companion. *Nope*, he thought. *Can't be half-bad at all.*

Strawberry Fest, held in an open area near the beach on Harbor Light's east end, had a carnival-like atmosphere. The duo started along the midway and rode the Tilt-A-Whirl; the bumper cars; the Teacups. As they started toward one of the food carts, where you could get everything-on-a-stick, Donovan's hand brushed against Lisa's. A warm sensation drifted up his belly. He took out his Super High Bouncy Ball for a few hits on the ground. Dessert consisted of ice cream cones: chocolate for him; pistachio for her. They decided to enjoy them while taking a stroll on the boardwalk.

"Is it hard?" she asked. "You know. Being small."

"Yeah, I guess." Donovan wasn't quite ready to spill the beans regarding his recent adventures in pharmacology. "Some kids can be pretty mean."

"Yeah, I know. Especially that bitch, Farrah LaCroix." He was slightly taken aback at Lisa's swearing. Donovan never swore. "She has everything most girls want. Money, looks. I wonder why she hangs around those losers."

"I guess when it comes to meanness," he said, "like really does attract like." They both chuckled. Their hands again brushed against each other. This time, Donovan took hers in his. His knees became weak for a second when she reciprocated the clasp. He turned his head to look at her. "Is money something *you* want?"

"No. Money doesn't impress me." Donovan was relieved to hear that, considering that he and his family had little in the bread department.

Ice cream finished, they were back on the midway, walking slowly (still holding hands) toward the exit. As they started to make their way along a row of carnival games, Donovan noticed a loud, high-pitched voice: "STEP RIGHT UP, FOLKS! STEP RIGHT UP! WIN A PRIZE! WHO'S THE MARKSMAN? WHO'S THE SHARPSHOOTER?" He then beheld the man behind the voice. He was wearing a white button-down shirt, with black slacks and a black bow tie. With his small black mustache and black hair parted sharply on the left, Donovan thought he looked every bit the vintage carnival barker.

Lisa stopped.

"Awww! Look how pretty that is!" she said, pointing a finger. Beyond Mr. Bow Tie, Donovan saw a huge stuffed pink unicorn with a candy-striped horn.

"STEP RIGHT UP, YOUNG MAN! WIN YOUR SWEETHEART AN ADORABLE PRIZE THAT'LL MAKE HER LOVE YA TILL THE END OF TIME!"

Donovan looked at Lisa and noticed the color rise in her cheeks. He absolutely had to win that unicorn. The two walked over to Mr. Bow Tie, Donovan going right up to the ledge, where an air pistol, fastened by a cord to the wooden ledge and loaded with a cork projectile, was resting.

"Nice to meetcha! I'm Gabe the Gamer, young man, Gabe the Gamer!"

Donovan saw a board behind Mr. Bow Tie— Gabe—that had a clown's head painted on it. A white face with bright red lips and a bright red nose. In the center of the clown's open laughing mouth was a hole that he believed was just barely wider than the cork. "I'm Donovan. Nice to meet you. What are the rules?"

"Rules rules rules are for shmoolz it's very simple my dear friend Donovan for a buck a shot you shoot the cork in the hole and win your girl a prize deuces aces one-eyed faces wha'dya say? Who's the marksman? Who's the sharpshooter?"

Donovan knew from the change he received from the ice cream vendor that he had exactly four dollars to his name. He looked up at the prizes. They were all stuffed animals, several small ones on the right and a few large ones on the left, including the pretty unicorn. "Win two small ones and you can trade up for a big one. Wha'dya say young man? Who's the marksman? Who's the sharpshooter?"

"Okay." Donovan pulled a dollar out of his wallet and gave it to the gamer.

"Alright let's see whatcha got kiddo."

Donovan picked up the pistol with a one-handed nervous grip and rather carelessly pulled the trigger. The cork hit the board no where near the clown's mouth.

"That's okay, Donovan," Lisa said. "At least you tried."

"Try again young man try again win your girl a prize." The wild shot made Donovan recall a memory from the previous fall.

He had asked his dad permission to go handgun shooting at the McAllister farm. Joe Marsden, a gun owner himself, had given his enthusiastic approval. He was just glad his son wanted to do something manly for a change, instead of reading those sissy science books. Ralph McAllister, Rodney's dad, had taken the kids out back to the homemade range to give them instruction. Rodney had shot before. This was more-or-less a refresher for him. Donovan, though, had never discharged a firearm.

Alright, boys, Ralph (in his bib overalls and a green John Deere ball cap) said. *Here are some fundamentals.* He picked up the .22-caliber Smith & Wesson semi-automatic. *Always keep the safety on and your finger outside the trigger guard until you're ready to fire. You grip the firearm like so, like you're shakin a fella's hand. Your other hand reinforces the grip from underneath like so. This bead here is the front sight. This notch here is the rear sight.* Standing approximately fifteen feet from a basic paper target with black circles, Ralph pointed. Switched off the safety. *Put the target to the bead and the bead to the notch. And boys, don't hold your breath when you fire. You slowly, calmly exhale when you fire.* He then placed his index finger inside the trigger guard. *And, boys, this is very important. You don't pull the trigger. You* squeeeeze *the trigger.* Ralph squeezed the trigger. The noise startled Donovan. The three of them walked over to the target. It was a perfect bull's-eye.

Donovan took out another dollar.

"That's what I like ta see that's what I like ta see win a prize."

This time, Donovan used the reinforced grip taught to him by Ralph McAllister. He put the target to the bead and the bead to the notch. He took a deep breath in. Placed his finger on the trigger.

Exhaled.

Squeezed.

And missed.

"Oooh! You almost had it young man try again try again."

"Let's go, Donovan," Lisa said. "It's just a stuffed animal."

The cork hit about a half-inch to the left of and an inch above the target. *The sighting's off,* he thought. He wasn't the type (nor did he have the courage) to call shenanigans. He'd simply make the proper adjustments. He *needed* that unicorn.

Donovan took out another dollar.

"That's what I like ta see that's what I like ta see take another shot." Gabe the Gamer loaded another cork.

Now, Donovan aimed dead center. Then, half an inch to the right. An inch down. And fired.

When the cork projectile sailed perfectly through the clown's mouth-hole, Gabe the Gamer's jaw literally dropped. Donovan detected not only surprise in his expression (as if this was the first successful shot made all day), but also fear. *Afraid I'm going to clean you out, huh Gabe?* "Yayyy!" Lisa screamed.

"Holy cow! That's great shootin young man great shootin which one do ya want?" Gabe the Gamer was reaching toward the smaller prizes.

Donovan took out his last dollar.

"I'm going for the unicorn, Gabe."

"Hey. Yeah. Why not? Sometimes lightning strikes twice, right?" Gabe looked worried.

Donovan, seemingly without effort, sank the final cork through the hole. "Oh my!" Lisa jumped. "You did it! You did it!"

A defeated Gabe the Gamer pulled down the unicorn and gave it to the winner. "Congratulations, young man. That's some excellent shootin. Sad to say I gotta cutcha off. One big prize per shooter. Dems da rules dems da rules."

"'Rules are for shmoolz, right Gabe?" Donovan gave a coy, slightly sarcastic smile. "That's okay. I'm done." Lisa put a vise-like hug around his neck.

"You kiddos take care enjoy that unicorn great shootin great shootin."

As they were leaving, Donovan again heard the high-pitched voice behind him: "STEP RIGHT UP, FOLKS! WHO'S THE MARKSMAN? WHO'S THE SHARPSHOOTER?"

25

Alec Wilde returned to the office after a late lunch and looked at the afternoon's schedule:

2:30—Ramona Hall—Diabetes/Hypertension Follow-Up
2:45—Jesus Ramirez—Sore Throat
3:00—Robert Carter—Annual Check-Up
3:15—Arthur Mellinger—New Patient Consultation/Physical Exam

At 3:18, he entered one of two exam rooms in his small office, and beheld an older gentleman wearing rimless glasses and a tan fedora. "Misterrr Mellinger? Hard or soft g?"

"Hello, Dr. Wilde. Soft. You got it right. And please, call me Art."

"Well then, I guess you can call me Alec." The two shook hands, and Alec occupied the chair directly facing Art. "I must admit, it's a bit odd to see a new patient who resides in Wisconsin. Not exactly a stone's throw away. What brings you to Harbor Light?"

"Uh, research. It's been awhile since I've had a physical. I'll be in town for a few days, so I figured now was as good a time as any."

Alec glanced at the intake form. "Seventy-four years old, six feet one, one hundred sixty-two pounds. No medications?"

"I'm a research chemist. I know what's in those pharmaceuticals. I don't take anything unless I absolutely have to."

"Can't blame you there. Well, let's have a look." Alec opened his doctor bag and commenced the exam. Towards the end, while he was palpating his patient's abdomen, Alec said, "Art, you're a research chemist, but it states on the intake that you're also retired. Are you studying something informally?"

Art sat up and began to button his shirt. "Well, Doctor, Alec, I'll be entirely honest. There's an additional reason why I wanted to see you today. A far more important reason." Alec closed his bag and sat down in his chair. "Until recently, I was employed by Braxton-Wentworth Pharmaceuticals. I resigned due to possible ethical violations of the company. Possible legal violations. Perhaps a cover-up. I don't know yet. I've just recently started investigating. It has to do with the drug, Restor."

26

A lec sat on his living room sofa, paying no attention to the news on TV. He felt that if there ever was a time he needed a drink, it was now. But he stuck with Pepsi. Since Arthur Mellinger was his last appointment of the day, he agreed to accompany his new (patient?) acquaintance to his room at the Sheraton for a little palaver. After all, he had a patient that he'd placed on Restor, and he was curious as to what the research chemist had to say. At home now, Alec took a long draw from his pop, swallowed slowly, and recalled how Art had told his story, uninterrupted:

You've heard of Operation Ranch Hand and the rainbow herbicides used in Vietnam (not quite a question). *On behalf of the Air Force, I developed a chemical compound that was the main ingredient of the original formula for Agent Yellow. The compound was called Spharion A. Along with Agent Orange, Agent Yellow was one of the most effective defoliants used in South Vietnam in the mid-sixties. Then, we became aware of...*complications. *Complications that were directly attributable to Spharion A.*

We discovered acts of violence among villagers along the tracks where Agent Yellow was sprayed. A boy and his sister were playing on the roof of their hut.

According to a witness, he deliberately threw her off, and she landed on her head. She died with a crushed skull. When asked why he did it, he couldn't give an answer. He said he didn't remember doing it. A woman attacked her husband with a machete while he slept. His abdomen was mutilated, but he survived. Again, when questioned, she could give no response. She said she must have had a blackout. There was another boy. Twelve years old, good-natured and sociable with the other children in his village. His friends began to notice that he was becoming withdrawn. Isolated. Some of them found a shallow grave of dead animals just outside the boy's living quarters. Chickens; cats. One day, he broke into the home of a friend, a girl his own age. He strangled her and stripped off her clothes, post-mortem. He then removed his own clothes, broke a bottle on the floor, and shoved the jagged end into his neck, slicing the jugular. He collapsed on the girl and died. All of these events occurred where Agent Yellow was used.

It was clear to me that Spharion A, somehow, caused a psychological devolution among some in the population. The data, however, wasn't entirely conclusive. So the military simply chose to reformulate the agent, instead of owning up to any responsibility. The new formula, though, wasn't nearly as effective as the original, and Agent Yellow was shortly done away with altogether. In my final report regarding Spharion A, I happened to mention that those who had both been exposed to the chemical and suffered napalm burns, demonstrated a remarkable recovery. Under other circumstances I would have followed-up with that finding. But, as you can imagine, I just wanted to be done with Spharion A. To bury it forever.

After a long career, I retired from the military and began working for Braxton-Wentworth Pharmaceuticals in 1994. As part of their extensive background personnel investigations, they discovered my work with Spharion A and the incredible healing of the napalm victims. Even though my report was classified, Braxton's influence runs deep. The company wanted to embark on a trials process with the compound, formerly known as Spharion A, and third-degree burn victims. They asked me to monitor the situation. I realized the precarious situation I was in. I could refuse, and be completely shut out, ignorant of any possible negative outcomes. Or I could oversee the project and police it with strict vigilance. I agreed to their offer on the condition that the operation would be canceled at the first sign of trouble. They accepted.

Upon FDA approval, the experimentations went flawlessly. The resulting drug, Restor, was first administered to American and allied forces burn victims in the Middle East. Then stateside. Then worldwide. The patients experienced an immense degree of healing with only a low level of potential side effects.

As a practicing physician, Alec, you're probably aware that a drug's patent expires after twenty years. At that point, generics, copycats, can be made and prescribed at a much lower cost to the consumer. Restor's patent is set to expire in 2021. Braxton-Wentworth started to panic about that a few years ago. Then, a research analyst in the company hypothesized that Restor could be used effectively for those with certain growth disorders, specifically idiopathic short stature. You see, a drug's patent can be renewed if a "new indication" for the drug is found. The company wants idiopathic short stature to be Restor's "new indication" before 2021. In the meantime, it's encouraging doctors to prescribe the drug off-label for the disorder in order to convince the government of its efficacy and gain approval.

The company asked me to supervise Restor's off-label usage. I agreed, conditionally. Again, I gave them my stipulation that if anything went awry, the prescribing would stop. Again, they accepted.

The children who were diagnosed with ISS and given Restor responded phenomenally. And there didn't seem to be any noticeable side effects. And then...it started happening. A shooting in Miami. A self-mutilation in Roanoke. I brought this to the company's attention and demanded that the prescribing cease. They refused. They claimed that there was no solid evidence that Restor was to blame. So, I resigned in protest. I made copies of synopses of some of the horrific events. I also have a list of physicians who have prescribed Restor for ISS. I want to personally investigate these tragedies, and warn the doctors about the medication. You're the first doctor I've met with.

Alec, here's the thing. None of the burn victims experienced negative effects. Only when the drug is prescribed off-label do these horrible psychological consequences occur. And that's only among a small population of the patients. Why do some suffer from *these effects, and others, the overwhelming majority, do not? There has to be a link; a common denominator. That's what I'm determined to find out.*

27

"Jesus, Art."

"Pretty intense, huh?"

They were sitting in Art's single-room hotel suite, Alec on a chair in the corner, Art on one of the twin beds. Alec opened his mouth to speak. Once; twice. Finally, "What are you going to do next?"

Art adjusted the fedora he was still wearing. "I'm going to head out to Roanoke tomorrow morning. Speak with the victim, his family, and try to meet with the prescribing physician." Art read the expression on Alec's face. "Look, Alec, I can tell you're a compassionate physician. You're concerned about your patient."

"I was really hoping that Restor could help him. He's such a sweet boy."

"I fully intend to investigate these situations, turn over what I find to the FDA, and have Restor's off-label use stopped. In the meantime…I trust your best clinical judgment."

"I appreciate that, Art, but you don't even know me."

"I know enough."

28

Alec had been looking forward to the thirteenth of July, Donovan's first follow-up, since his conversation with Art a couple weeks ago. Donovan sat in the exam room awaiting his doctor, dressed only in his underwear and a patient gown.

"Good morning, Donovan."

"Good morning, Dr. Wilde. How are you?"

general appearance: moderate acne, mildly slouched posture

"Fine. Fine. Step on up to the scale. How's your summer going?"

height: 5 ft

"It's going great! I'm helping out Coach Barrison with the football team and my friend Rodney got me a job at the library where he works."

weight: 97 lbs

"Good, good. Have a seat on the table, young man. Are you having any fun? Swimming?"

"Yeah, Rodney and I go to the beach sometimes. And I took Lisa to Cedar Point."

heart/lung auscultation: unremarkable

"Lisa?"

"Lisa Bailey."

blood pressure: 116/74

pulse: 62

"Oh yeah, Mike and Lola's daughter. Open up and put this under your tongue. I'm going to push on your tummy. Let me know if any of this hurts."

"Um-kay."

abdominal palpation: unremarkable

temperature: 98.7 f

respiration: 12

"So is Lisa your girlfriend?"

"I don't know. I guess she's my girlfriend. I really like her a lot."

"Well, I'm sure she's a very sweet girl since she has your attention. Any pain in your privates?"

"Nope."

"Any headaches? Back or neck pain? Arm or leg pain?"

"Nope."

"Okay, then. Go ahead and put your clothes back on and meet me in my office."

Alec explained to Donovan again that it might take some more time before he experienced results from the medication. The doctor was relieved that, at least for the moment, there were no negative effects from the drug on his patient. Maybe Art was wrong about Restor. Maybe those horrible things that had happened was just coincidence. Maybe the drug would work for Donovan with no adverse effects at all. Maybe.

PART TWO

METAMORPHOSIS

1

That summer, Donovan was the happiest he had ever been. He worked with Rodney at the library, and afterwards they would do what typical teenaged boys do for fun. He worked with the football team as weight room coordinator and head waterboy. He continued with his exercising and jujitsu training with Coach Barrison. And, of course, he spent quality time with Lisa.

Donovan woke up on a mid-August Sunday, having slept in. It was a free day. The library was closed and he had no football duties. Per his usual custom, he slumbered out of bed, went to the bathroom, brushed his teeth, and showered. As he walked back into his bedroom with a white towel wrapped around his torso, he caught a glimpse of himself in the mirror. He turned to face the mirror straight on. Donovan had never liked looking at a reflection of his body. He was embarrassed by it. But now, the image that was staring back at him didn't appear to be his. It appeared to be someone else. Someone *better*. He could see his abdominal muscles, forming into an impressive six-pack. His chest was becoming sculpted and defined. He could see veins coursing along his biceps and forearms. A feeling of bemusement came over him. He didn't see his best friend walk into the room.

"Whoa! Dude!"

"Hey, Rodney."

"Man, I knew you were starting to fill out your clothes, but I didn't know you looked like *this*. You've gotten a lot taller too."

"Yeah, I started noticing that a few weeks ago."

"Looks like that medication is starting to work."

"Yeah. And the workouts with Coach Barrison."

"If I wasn't such a geek, I'd ask you to train me."

"We're both geeks, Rodney. The geek squad to the end. You and me. That's what we've always said."

2

D r. Alec Wilde checked his schedule for this Tuesday morning, September 4. Cluster-booking is the term used when appointments are bunched together in a short frame of time, giving the appearance that the practice is busier than it actually is. While this helps, the truth was, Alec spent most of his time in his office reading mystery novels. He had a loyal base, and he loved caring for his patients, but he was doing little more than keeping his head above water. Apparently, just as many potential patients were repelled by his former mid-level regional celebrity status (and subsequent downfall) as were attracted to it.

9:00—Linda Butler—Abdominal Discomfort

Linda Butler. And she would undoubtedly bring that asshole husband of hers, George.

Alec used the bathroom before starting his work day. The mild burning sensation he had barely noticed a few days ago while he urinated was becoming more pronounced. Probably the onset of a urinary tract infection, he surmised. Drinking too much coffee and Pepsi and not enough water didn't help. Maybe he would have it checked out by Kimberly Middleton. Kimberly had been one of his interns at the Cleveland

Clinic back in the day. She now had a primary care practice in Vermilion, with an in-house lab.

Dr. Wilde gave two knocks on the exam room door and walked in. "Linda, George. How are you this morning?"

"Okay, I guess," George said. "Linda here, uh, slipped and fell down the stairs yesterday. I guess she's, uh, a little clumsy. Right, honey?"

"Right." Linda was sitting on the table with her head down and arms folded in front, wearing a blue examination gown.

"Well, let's take a look," Alec said. He observed her overall appearance and demeanor and examined her midsection, while making small talk with the couple. Well, it was George who was talking.

The doctor certainly noticed a discoloration in the area (along with other marks about her body). It seemed, however, that it was far more likely caused by something like, say, a fist than a stair step. Alec had seen this type of rodeo before.

Multiple bruises at various stages of healing.

Demure, passive disposition.

Protective posture.

Husband does all the speaking (and excuse-making).

"Well, I think we can rule out any organ damage," Alec said. "It seems like just a muscle strain. Take it easy over the next few days, Linda, and you should start feeling better."

"Aren't you gonna give her somethin for pain?" George (whom Alec knew was rumored around town as a pill-head) said.

"I don't think so. Linda, if you feel the need to take a pain reliever, then something like Aleve that you can get at the local CVS should work just fine."

"I don't know, Doc. She looks pretty bad."

"Aleve should work just fine. Linda, while you're getting dressed, do you mind if I borrow your husband for a sec to talk about some guy stuff?"

"Okay," she muttered.

3

In the last weeks of summer break, in addition to his physique filling out and getting taller, other changes were made to Donovan's appearance. After three years of wearing braces on his teeth, they were finally removed. He thought his mouth felt funny without them, but he loved his new smile. During his annual eye exam, he opted for contacts instead of a new pair of glasses. He initially found it impossible to get the lenses on his eyeballs, but he got the hang of it after a few tries. He also decided to change his hair-style. Forgoing the hard part on the left that he had since he could remember, he now sported a more hip, slightly spiky do.

Indeed, during the morning of his first day back to school, many of his fellow students didn't know who Donovan was. Some just assumed he was an import (Harbor Light High slang for a transfer student). Donovan was relieved. A fresh start.

During third-period study hall, Donovan decided to go to the weight room and tidy up. Although he was no longer on the school's payroll, he had become well-acquainted with the players over the summer, and wanted to help out as much as possible. Upon arrival, he noticed that Chad Chandler and Bryan Winston (the Panthers' starting quarterback and halfback, respectively) had also decided to cut study hall to come here and shoot the breeze.

"Hey, Marsden," Chad (whose modern-day hippie parents had thought it was just grand and hilarious to name their first-born child, Chandler Chandler) said. "Bry and I are going fishing after practice at West Pier. Wanna join us?"

"Yeah," Bryan said. "Three's company."

"Really?"

"Yeah," Chad replied. "You gotta rod and tackle?"

Donovan thought about his father's ancient fishing equipment in the shed that hadn't been touched in years. "Yeah, I have some stuff."

"Well then, meet up with us at the pier at five," Chad said.

Bryan nodded.

Donovan felt a wave of euphoria wash over him. He couldn't believe it. They invited *him* to hang out with *them*? The two most popular guys in the school. *I'm nothing; a nobody. Yet* they *want to hang out with* me. Donovan remembered that he had plans with Rodney this afternoon to play with Rodney's G.I. Joe collection. Although well into their teens, they still loved playing with the G.I. Joe stuff once in awhile. But how could he turn down Chad's and Bryan's offer? This might be a chance. A chance to maybe get elevated from nothingness to their clique. Certainly Rodney would understand if he told him that he just couldn't make it over today. Sure he would.

"Okay," Donovan said.

4

George Butler closed the door after following Alec into his office. "What's up, Doc?"

"I'll tell you what's up, you son of a bitch," Alec said as he stood behind his desk with his fists on the top. "If I ever see your wife in that condition again, I'll call the authorities. I'd do it right now if I had more proof."

"Proof of what?" George countered with a raised voice. He folded his arms over his now puffed-out chest. Alec had heard that George, who was the lead mechanic at Harbor Light Toyota, had a lightning-quick temper.

"Cut the shit!" Alec said, his voice now barely above a whisper. "Keep getting pilled-up and slapping her around, and you'll go down."

George clenched his fists, but then seemed to cower.

"I ain't done nothin. Y-You sure are one to talk about...intoxication. Don't think I ain't heard about it."

Alec stared into his shifty brown eyes.

"Linda and me...we'll just get ourselves a new doctor. You ain't shit."

"Get the hell out of here," Alec said with a snarl.

5

After a fairly enjoyable first day at school, Donovan arrived at West Pier just before five. While walking to the edge of the pier with his father's pole and tackle box, he noticed that Chad was sitting alone with his line in the water. "Hey, Chad," he said, then looked around. "Where's Bryan?"

"Oh, Bryan couldn't make it," Chad replied. "His dad made him mow the lawn."

Donovan sat down in the chair next to him. "Catch anything yet?"

"Nope, I just got here. Let's see what ya got."

Donovan opened up his box and displayed the typical items: lures, hooks, line, sinkers, artificial worms, etc. "It's been awhile since I've been fishing," he said. "Anything you'd recommend?" Chad glanced inside the box, gave it a once-over, and shook his head.

"Here, I'll share mine." Chad reached under his chair, picked up a Styrofoam cup, and removed the plastic lid. Donovan saw worms squirming around in black soil. Chad picked one out and began to thread it onto Donovan's hook. "These tend to work the best. Minnows too. Usually catch perch and walleye. Sheephead are the most fun because they give you a good fight when you reel them in. You're all set." Donovan cast his line into Lake Erie.

"How was your first day back?" Chad asked as he twitched his head, clearing his Robert Kennedy-esque brown hair away from his eyes.

"It was okay. Seems like a lot of kids didn't know who I was. Teachers, too."

"Yeah, you sure have changed over the summer. Those workouts with Coach Barrison are paying off. You've gotten a lot taller, too."

"Yeah, my doctor put me on a medication to help me grow. I guess it's working."

"I'll say." Chad reeled his line in and attached a new worm to his hook. "Homecoming's comin up. You goin?"

"Oh. I haven't thought about it. I usually don't go to things like that." Donovan held his rod in his left hand, and his trusty Super High Bouncy Ball in his right. "I don't seem to fit in."

"I'm not that excited about going, myself. But, as starting quarterback, I guess I'm expected to go. Tell ya what, I'll go if you go."

"Okay."

"I suppose I'll take Wendy. Wendy Marshall. I lot of people think we're boyfriend/girlfriend, but we're not. We're just friends."

"I thought you were boyfriend/girlfriend too." Donovan felt a nibble on his fishing pole.

"Who do you think you'll ask?"

Without hesitation, Donovan said, "Lisa Bailey. I guess we're boyfriend/girlfriend, but I don't think we've made it official yet."

"Oh yeah, Lisa. She seems like a great girl."

"She's wonderful." Donovan smiled.

"Think we'll beat Port Clinton—? Oh, wow! Reel it in! Reel it in!"

Suddenly, Donovan's pole bent so far towards his hand, he thought the pole would snap in two.

"Bring it in nice and steady," Chad said. "Not too fast. I'll get the net."

It took everything Donovan had to keep turning the crank on his reel. "Not…gonna…let you get away," he grunted.

Chad saw the silhouette just below the water's surface. "Wow! It's a monster! Don't bring it out of the water; it might come off. Just keep it there; I'll scoop it out."

Chad leaned over the cement ledge with his staff and captured the fish in its netting, almost falling into the lake in the process. Donovan, with bared teeth and shaking arms, tried his best to maintain. Chad then plopped their prize catch down at their feet. "Man, I think that's the biggest sheephead I ever saw!" he said. "Congratulations on catching Moby Dick. You're alright, Marsden." They gave each other a high-five.

Donovan beamed.

6

The burning sensation had gotten worse.

You need to drink more water, Dr. Alec Wilde kept saying to himself as he sat in Dr. Kimberly Middleton's exam room. *Whatever caused this UTI, the caffeine has made it worse. More water and less Pep—*

There were two raps at the door before it opened.

"Alec!"

"Kimberly!" They embraced.

"You have quite an office here," Alec said. "Welcome to family practice."

"Yeah, it's certainly an adventure," Kimberly replied. "We get to see everything. Speaking of which…"

"I know, I know. 'Physician, heal thyself.' I promise I'll cut down on the pop and coffee after we get this UTI fixed." He crossed his fingers on both hands and winked.

"Okay, then," she chuckled. "I suppose you know what to do with this—." She handed him a plastic cup. "Bathroom's on the right."

Forty-five minutes later, Alec glanced at his watch. He was thinking that Kimberly must be having a busy day.

A moment later, Dr. Middleton knocked on the door and entered. She had a look on her face that Alec had never seen while she'd interned under him.

A look of concern.

"Oh, no," Alec said with a grin. "Let me guess. You're going to ban me from soft drinks for life."

Kimberly pulled up a chair directly across from him and sat down.

"Alec," she said carefully. Worriedly. "I don't know how to tell you this—you have chlamydia."

Kimberly's words didn't immediately register with Alec. Chlamydia? An STD? But, that can't be. He'd always been faithful to—

Emily.

He lowered his head, shut his eyes, and exhaled. "Looks like there'll be an interesting conversation tonight at the Wilde residence," he said. "At least it was great seeing you again, Doc."

"I'm so sorry," was all Kimberly could offer. "It was great seeing you again, too. I'll write you a script."

7

Route 6 is the second-longest federal highway in the continental US, stretching from California to Massachusetts. In Harbor Light, it borders Lake Erie (and is known locally as Shoreline Drive) and serves as the town's main drag.

On the same warm, cloudless afternoon Alec Wilde learned that the fire emanating from his penis was *not* the result of a caffeine-exacerbated UTI, Donovan Marsden pulled into the Circle K gas station on Shoreline. The beautiful weather belied Alec's day—and now—Donovan's.

Donovan pulled along the west side of the building, next to the air compressor. Just moments ago, the indicator light on the Fusion's dashboard had warned him of a low tire. (He'd thought the left front tire looked a little deflated when he'd left school that day.) He slid off the seat (noting proudly that he no longer had to use a cushion underneath him in order to see through the windshield) and began putting quarters into the machine.

On the north side of the building, Ted Mullins was refueling his dull red 1990s-version Camaro. His sidekicks this afternoon consisted of a couple of other winners: Vic Morey and Toby Butler. Ted lit up a Marlboro. Yes. He was a king and the world was his ashtray. Fuck it if he was smoking next to a gas pump. Ted wasn't really sweatin life since he'd "dropped out" of school. Between working odd jobs and mooching off his mom, he was getting by. Besides, Toby's old man said he could get him a job at Harbor Light Toyota. He'd have to get a GED first, though. He was thinking about what he was going to get messed up on tonight (Budweiser or Jack Daniel's) when—

"No fuckin way," Vic and Toby heard Ted say.

"What is it?" Vic said.

"I think I know that little prick." Vic and Toby strained their necks from inside the car in Ted's line of sight, glimpsing the blond boy who was putting air in his tire. "He manned-up a little since, but yeah...yeah, that's him. C'mon, boys, let's have some fun."

I hope this holds, Donovan thought as he replaced the cap on the tire valve. *I don't really have the money for a new tire, and Dad made it clear that I'm responsible for all the maintenance. Maybe I can use one of those fix-a-flat thingies—*

"Y'know, I thought you woulda left town after the last beat-down."

From his squatting position, Donovan looked up to the sunshine and the feathered mullet that was caught in it. He instantly knew who it belonged to. *Oh, no.*

"Ya think you're a stud because ya got bigger?" Ted mockingly squeezed Donovan's upper arm twice with his thumb and middle finger. "You're stilla little pussy."

Donovan stood up and took a step back. Toby then kicked a small stone at him. As Donovan's eyes went to it, Ted slapped him hard across the cheek.

It would be the only strike he'd pull off.

Donovan continued to walk backwards. He placed his arms in the defensive on-guard position taught to him by Coach Barrison, with elbows held in at chest level and palms together. The arrangement of the arms was deceptive. It gave the impression of submissiveness, while protecting the body's centerline and enabling a quick counterattack.

Ted followed.

The four were now behind Donovan's car, completely out of sight of the other patrons at the station.

Donovan's eyes welled with tears. But, unlike all the other times he had been bullied throughout his life: the slaps; the punches; the pushing; the verbal taunts— the tears weren't borne out of *fear*. They were brought on by *anger*.

No more, he thought.

No more beatings.

No more insults.

No more harassment.

"Aww, ya gonna cry, you little fucking pansy?" Ted said. "I'll give ya somethin to cry about."

"I...I'm warning you. Stay away from me."

"Hahahaha! *You're* warning *me*!"

Ted lunged and Donovan immediately sprang into action. Per Coach Barrison's jujitsu training, he jumped up, wrapped his legs around his opponent's midsection, and grasped his collar with both hands. Using Ted's forward momentum against him, the two landed on the pavement—with Ted on top.

Exactly where Donovan wanted him.

"I'm gonna kill you, bitch!" Ted screamed.

In one fluid motion, Donovan braced Ted's left shoulder and arm from below with his hands, brought his right leg around Ted's face, and using his upper thigh as a fulcrum...*squeeeeezed.*

And dislocated Ted's elbow.

"Owwww! Sonofabitch!"

Donovan scrambled to his feet. Toby Butler and Vic Morey were momentarily stunned stiff with mouths agape, trying to decipher what they had just witnessed. Donovan utilized that opportunity to jump in his car, start the engine, and speed away. As he drove home, his heart pounded and he was filled with a myriad of emotions.

8

Alec sat alone at the dining room table, coddling his Pepsi—resisting the urge to coddle something stronger. He contemplated the day's events. Contemplated his marriage. Sure, he had suspected that maybe Emily was running around on him. Suspected. But, he'd always given her the benefit of the doubt. Em cheating on him was almost inconceivable. But, now he had the conclusive proof; the kind of proof that required antibiotics to eliminate. He sat there pondering his options.

Emily came home shortly after six-thirty with take-out from Marsha's Pizzeria. "Hey, Alec. How was your day?" (They'd stopped using pet names such as *hon* and *sweetie* long ago.)

"Funny you should ask."

"Oh?" She served portions of spaghetti, subs, and garlic bread onto plates and set one in front of her husband. He didn't have an appetite.

"Em…Emily…do you have something to tell me?" He looked her in the eyes, trying to be stoic through his grief.

"Christ, Alec, I've had a long day. If you have something to say, then just say it." She stuck a forkful of spaghetti in her mouth and eyed her food from her seat at the head of the table.

"I saw Kimberly Middleton today. She was very generous in kindly informing me that I had contracted chlamydia."

Emily stopped chewing. Swallowed. "You—"

"No," he interrupted. "I never cheated on you. This is on you, Em."

She continued with her downward gaze.

"I won't ask you who it was. Or was it several people?"

She continued with her downward gaze.

"I'm not surprised you didn't know," his voice now more stern. "Chlamydia is typically asymptomatic in women." Emily opened her mouth to speak. Closed it.

"I'll save you the embarrassment that I went through. I got Z-packs for both of us." Alec slammed her supply of azithromycin on the table in front of her.

Forty seconds of silence elapsed.

"I've decided to leave for awhile," he finally said.

She looked up at him. He now had his head down.

"Where will you go?"

"I don't know. A hotel somewhere. I'll let you know when I get there."

"For how long?"

"I don't know."

"Alec—"

"Don't. Don't, Em. I suppose both of us need some time apart to…think about things." With that, Alec stood up from the table and started for the bedroom to pack.

Emily wept.

9

Diary entry of Donovan Marsden
dated September 12, 2018

I 'm still breathing hard from what happened today. I can't believe my parents didn't notice anything wrong during dinner. Ted Mullins came at me. I stayed calm, well, as calm as I could, and reacted the way Jermaine taught me. I think I broke Ted's arm. I really do. The question now is what will become of it? Will they leave me alone, or will they double-down on picking on me? Maybe they'll try to do something a lot worse than what I did to Ted. I don't know. I guess I'll just wait and see. Mikey wanted to play catch after dinner, but I was still too jazzed up to do anything other than sit in my room and think. I feel bad about not playing with Mikey. I'll make it up to him tomorrow. Anyway, I have another follow-up with Dr. Wilde in a couple days. I hope he'll like how much I've grown. I sure like how much I've grown. Time for bed. I hope I can sleep. Goodnight.

10

A lec was in his office documenting patient files. Actually, he was doing more thinking than documenting.

His initial inclination the other night had been to leave Harbor Light (leave Erie County) and stay someplace where no one would know him. Somewhere, a big city, that would allow him to be anonymous. Hide.

But then he'd changed his mind. He missed the small-town atmosphere of his childhood. Maybe getting back to his roots would give him a much-welcomed, much-needed, relief. And with fall coming up, the scenery would be wonderful. He'd always loved the autumn environment of his youth. So, he'd decided to check in at the Country Hearth Inn in Willard, which was close (but not too close) to his hometown. He'd have to drive about forty-five minutes north every morning to get to work, but that was okay. Perhaps the daily drive time would do him some good.

He called Emily that night after he got settled in. She again asked him how long he'd be gone. He again said that he didn't know. What he did know, or thought he knew, was that some time apart would be therapeutic for both of them. They'd been stuck together over the whirlwind of the last few years, and so some solitude might be in order. Never mind that she had cheated on him (apparently with more than one guy).

Something else was clawing at his mind.

Donovan Marsden.

Jesus, I didn't even recognize the kid when I walked into the exam room today, he thought. He figured there must have been a scheduling error. Granted, some of the changes had been made on his own: a new hairstyle; lack of glasses. And his braces had been removed. And he was obviously lifting weights. But also, his acne has almost completely cleared. Most striking of all—he had grown almost two inches since his last appointment. That was two inches in two months! How was that even possible? To add to the astonishment, there didn't seem to be any negative side effects. His vitals were in normal range, he didn't report any pain or negative changes, and the examination didn't reveal anything suspect.

Alec was suspicious. As a practicing physician, he was well aware of the tremendous power of pharmacology. But the results that young Master Marsden was experiencing were just—too good to be true. Eventually, something would have to give. A drug couldn't have this much of an impact without causing one or more adverse effects. Major adverse effects, he surmised.

Restor.

His interest in the *miracle* drug rose to a new level. He decided to call Art Mellinger.

11

September 28, 2018

Homecoming Game: Sandusky Blue Streaks vs. Harbor Light Panthers

"Welcome back, sports fans, to WSWL, the home of good-time rock and roll oldies, and the home of the Sandusky Bay Conference. This is John Hall, with the legendary sportscaster, Mike Ackerman, and Mike, do we have a barnburner tonight."

"We sure do, John. Sandusky and Harbor Light are the biggest rivals in the conference, and this game has come right down to the wire."

"Although it's early in the season, both of these teams are undefeated, and both are expected to do *very* well this year. Here's the situation: both teams' incredible defense has kept this a low-scoring contest. With forty-eight seconds left in the game, the Blue Streaks have the ball at the Panthers' twenty-two-yard line. Sandusky is up seventeen to thirteen, and it seems that victory is theirs if they just hold on to the ball, Mike."

"That's right, John. And, even if Harbor Light reclaims the ball, with so little time left, they would need a touchdown to win. A field goal wouldn't be enough."

"The players line up on the field after a Sandusky timeout. Quarterback Jason Berry calls the play. Handoff to—FUMBLE! FUMBLE!"

"Oh, my!"

"Recovered by Panthers' tackle, number nineteen, Tim Busek! Panthers call a timeout! Fans, we'll be right back after these words from our sponsors…"

Below the press box, there was pandemonium in the Panthers' stands and on the sidelines. Donovan walked among the players with a tray of water bottles, offering hydration and words of encouragement. After a huddle broke between head coach Earl Reeves, Chad Chandler, Bryan Winston, and wide receiver Micah Stephens, he approached his friend. "You can do it, Chad."

"Thanks, Donovan. It's a long shot, but I'll try."

:41: First down. Chad hands off to Bryan, who is almost immediately brought down. The team scurries back to formation. They have no more timeouts left.

:29: Second down. Chad again hands off to Bryan, who's able to advance a few yards.

:18: Third down. Chad drops back, looking for a receiver. Looking. Looking. He doesn't think he'll gain any yardage by making a run for it. The Panthers' defensive wall does an excellent job of protecting their QB. Finally, a Blue Streaks linebacker breaks through and sacks Chad at the Panthers' nineteen-yard line.

:3: Fourth down. Chad drops back. Dodges the linebacker who tackled him the last play, making a hard right. Out of the corner of his eye, he sees a player darting into the endzone from the left. A player who wears the same jersey as his own. He launches the ball...it's caught...by Micah Stephens. TOUCHDOWN! GAME OVER!

12

The next morning, Donovan drove west with a multitude of emotions. He was exhausted from last night's post-game celebration, which had lasted into the wee hours of the morning. Earl Reeves had treated the boys to pizza and Cokes at his home. (Coach Reeves had turned a blind eye to the occasional splash of whiskey into the occasional cup of Coca-Cola.)

He was happy. Harbor Light had defeated (albeit narrowly) its chief rival, the Sandusky Blue Streaks, in the Panthers' homecoming game. His best friend—*Is Chad now my best friend?*—had made an amazing pass, and Micah made an amazing catch. And tonight was the homecoming dance.

He was excited. Yes, tonight was the homecoming dance. He and Lisa would be hanging out with the uber-popular guys and their uber-popular girlfriends. In a matter of weeks, Donovan had gone from one end of the social totem pole to the other. How had that happened? His dramatic physical transformation? A chance invitation to go fishing with Chad Chandler? The fact (although he was still very shy) that he now carried himself with more self-esteem? Donovan figured it was a combination of the three. He was looking forward to having fun at the dance. Rodney, of course, wouldn't be there. Rodney. He had been spending less and less time with his lifelong buddy. And he missed him. Donovan was glad that he and Rodney had separate lunch periods, so he wouldn't have to decide between sitting with Rodney and sitting with *the guys*. Rodney. He decided that he would stew over that situation later.

He was nervous. He and Lisa Bailey had been *dating* since the beginning of summer. They would hang out: talk; laugh; hold hands; sometimes neck. It was implied, by him anyway, that they were a couple. But, it had never been made official. He'd never asked her to *go steady*. (Was that term still even used?) He resolved to make it official tonight after the dance...with a present. Donovan had slyly scored her ring size the previous week, without her suspecting anything. He had an idea what he wanted to get her, and now he was on his way to Zales at the Sandusky Mall to see if they could accommodate him.

13

With Emily, Donovan Marsden, and Restor on his mind, Alec called Art Mellinger for a chat. Art informed Alec that he would be meeting with a family member of a possible Restor victim in the next couple of days, and invited him to join him. Alec accepted. He hadn't had any time off from work since his forced "vacation" a few years ago. Some time away from the office was just what the doctor ordered. He phoned Melanie, his office manager, and had her clear the following week's schedule.

On a dreary, overcast Tuesday morning, Alec and Art met at a diner thirty miles outside of South Bend, Indiana. They discussed the situation ahead.

"A fourteen-year-old girl shot her best friend with a twelve-gauge shotgun, almost killing her," Art said. "Then she put the gun to her head, and there was no almost about it."

"How long had she been on Restor?" Alec asked as he took a draw on his not-strong-enough black coffee.

"Five months," Art replied.

"My patient's been on it for over four months. Jesus."

The two men drove to a nearby farmhouse and met with Emma Higginbottom. The three of them took a stroll around her property.

"Even though Eve was a popular girl in school, she hated being so small," Emma said. "Herb and I tried to make her feel better about it, but it wouldn't do any good. Then one day our family doctor told us about Restor." She shot a brief sneer at Alec. "Our Evie had high hopes it would work."

"Did you notice any changes in Eve's behavior at first?" Art asked. They were walking the circumference of a large pond.

"Not at first. But then we started to notice that her moods were getting worse. She always had mood swings with her depression, but now they were getting... just...worse. And that nasty temper. She never had that before."

"Did you and your husband suspect that it was Restor?" Alec asked.

"No. We just figured she was going through a bad spell and that maybe we needed to change Eve's depression medication if it didn't pass."

Art adjusted his ever-present fedora and removed his glasses to clean the lenses. "Did Eve ever show signs of violence or suicidal tendencies?"

"No," Emma said, then frowned. "Not until the end. Her temper got worse and she started picking fights with her little sister. She got into some squabbles at school. After that, she just kinda withdrew. She would hardly talk with anyone, hardly communicate with anyone. She started missing days at school, even though she always had perfect attendance. A lot of times, Herb and I would catch Evie talking to herself. Mostly gibberish." Emma lowered her eyes to the locket around her neck that she was caressing. "Then one day her best friend Jill came over, as she so often did. Jill said they were sitting on the couch watching TV, eating candy. Eve calmly got up, left the room for a minute. When she returned, she had Herb's gun pointed right at Jill. She must have gotten it from underneath our bed. We didn't think the children knew where it was. Anyway. With no words shared, with no expression on her face, Eve shot Jill through her right shoulder. Then she racked in another shell, put the stock on the floor, put her mouth over the barrel, right toe on the trigger, and...and—"

"Mrs. Higginbottom, I'm so sorry—" Alec started.

"Please!" she interrupted. "Please. Spare me your condolences, gentlemen."

"Did Braxton-Wentworth contact you afterwards?" Art broke in.

"Yes. Someone who said he was with the company's 'outreach program' called about a week later, right after the funeral. He had a foreign accent—an oriental accent."

Alec didn't notice the twitch in Art's cheek at that moment.

"Anyway, he asked a few questions and that was that. Herb and I spoke with an attorney about taking action against Braxton-Wentworth, but we were told that with Eve's history of depression we wouldn't have a case. The company would just claim that her depression was to blame."

A minute of silence elapsed as the trio made their way back to the house. Abruptly, Emma stopped walking. Her short brown hair, etched with gray, tossed in the wind. "I know this for sure. That drug had everything to do with my daughter's...tragedy. Damn you for working for that company." She glared at Art. "And damn you for prescribing it." She glared at Alec. "I just hope that now you two can do something to stop it. No other family should have to deal with this.

"My Evie," she said, weeping now with both hands around the locket. "My poor Evie."

14

That afternoon, with the breaking sun now behind him, Alec was driving along I-70 East (an endless exhibit of silos and antique stores) on his way to Columbus. He was planning on catching a musical that evening in the city in order to lighten his mood; if that was even possible. Not long after crossing the Indiana-Ohio border, he remembered something about that morning's meeting with Emma Higginbottom. He called Art Mellinger from his cell phone.

"Art, Mrs. Higginbottom mentioned that she was contacted by an Asian gentleman—"

"Hiro Matsuda."

"Hero wha?"

"Hiro Matsuda," he repeated. "And he's no gentleman." Art was in his hotel room, packing up after a brief nap.

"How do you know him?"

"I don't. Some within the company claim he's a myth. But, from what I gather, he's very real. And he's not in some bogus outreach program. Apparently, Mr. Matsuda serves as BJ Wentworth's iron fist, in charge of stamping out negativity. And potential whistleblowers. Rumor has it that he's even killed one or two former company officials who threatened to leak potentially devastating information. Just rumors, of course."

Alec drove past a faded red barn. CHEW MAIL POUCH TOBACCO, the side of it read. "Art, you be careful."

"Oh, yes. I'm always careful, indeed. I have no doubts that Mr. Wentworth would like for me to disappear. I'm quite certain he knows what I'm up to. Who knows what lengths pharmaceutical companies will go to in order to protect their multi-billion-dollar crop?"

Alec nodded.

"By the way, Alec. I'll be checking out another case in Georgia next week. You're welcome to accompany me to that one as well."

"Thanks a lot, Art. I may very well take you up on the offer." The sky again turned gray.

15

Chad Chandler, Bryan Winston, and Donovan Marsden met up at the Sandusky Mall's food court at their agreed-upon time, just after Donovan's visit to Zales. The boys were munching heartily: Chad, kung pao chicken; Bryan, spaghetti with meatballs; Donovan, tacos. Their plan was to feast, then look for outfits for tonight's homecoming dance.

Whereas just a few months ago, Donovan would clearly have been the outcast among the group, now he easily fit in. Although much shorter than Chad and Bryan, his T-shirt sleeves filled out with muscles just like theirs did.

"Sweaters it is?" Chad asked.

"Sweaters it is," Bryan echoed.

"'Tis the season for sweaters," Donovan chimed in. "I guess summer's officially over."

Bryan looked down at the shiny black sack next to Donovan's foot. "Whatcha got in the bag?"

Donovan smiled and took a sip of his Mountain Dew. "A little something for Lisa after the dance."

Chad: "You guys going to any after-parties?"

Donovan: "Nah. I think we're going to hang out at West Pier."

"You're going parking at the beach?" Chad gave a sly grin.

"Con-sum-mate, con-sum-mate, con-sum-mate," Bryan chanted. All three boys broke out in laughter.

As they were emptying their trays into the trash bin, Donovan saw Rodney McAllister staring at him from the edge of the court. "Hey, guys, I'll be right back."

Donovan walked over to his old friend. "Hey, Rodney."

"Hey, Donovan."

Donovan noticed that Rodney's usual pep was absent. He struggled with what to say next. "Going to the dance tonight?"

Rodney exhaled a slight chuckle. "You know better than that." He gave a quick glance at Chad and Bryan. "Dude, what have you been up to? Outside of the library, I hardly ever see you anymore."

"Yeah." Donovan dropped his eyes to his nervous feet. "I've been really busy with the team, you know. And with Lisa. I'll call ya soon. We'll get together. Sound good?"

Rodney gave a faint smile. "Okay."

"Donovan!" one of the boys yelled. "Let's go! We're goin to Kohl's!"

"Well, I guess I have to go," Donovan said. "See ya."

"See ya."

16

Jermaine Barrison hadn't been out of his apartment much in the evenings since he and his girlfriend Yvonne had broken up last month. That was why he cheerfully accepted when he had been asked by the school administration to be one of the chaperones at the homecoming dance.

"This ravioli is wonderfully delicious." The only downside for Jermaine thus far was putting up with fat, weird Will Struthers, science and math instructor, talking his ear off at the unofficially designated teachers' table in the gym. "The wings are quite yummy, too," Mr. Struthers (who was working on his third plate) said. "You should try it, Mr. Barrison."

Outta sight, man, Jermaine thought. *This cat's outta sight.* Thankfully, the dance was winding down.

Jermaine was glad he had come. He was immensely impressed with how far his pupil Donovan had evolved. Besides raising his ten-year-old son Jamal, taking Donovan Marsden under his wing was the proudest endeavor of his adult life. It was simply amazing how far the boy had progressed in such a short amount of time. Not just physically, but also with his self-esteem and the way he now carried himself.

Jermaine knew that he couldn't take all the credit for Donovan's transformation. Some drug was responsible for the unreal growth spurt. And he knew that the young man might not be out of the woods as far as getting picked on by other kids. Attaining a new body brought problems of its own. He might need those self-defense skills now more than ever. Speaking of which—something going on four tables over caught Jermaine's eye.

It was no surprise that Chad Chandler had been elected homecoming king. (Bryan Winston's girlfriend, Molly Hay, won queen.) With the pageantry over, Chad, his lady friend Wendy Marshall, Bryan, Molly, Donovan, and Lisa sat at their table, dining on an assortment of tacos, chicken wings, cheese, and veggies.

"I don't know who's more fucking pathetic," Farrah LaCroix said as she approached the table, "this little geek or his puny, ugly-ass girlfriend." Her eyes bored into Donovan and Lisa. Farrah was standing next to her friend, Heather Mathews. (Not a close friend. Farrah didn't have close friends.)

"Shove off, Farrah," Lisa said.

"Watch your mouth, you little cunt," Farrah responded. "I'll add you to my list, along with your punk boyfriend."

Lisa, whose bravery and diction were five times the size of her petite frame, said, "It's strange seeing you without your flunkies hovering around you. Did you teach them how to sit and roll over yet?" The others at the table laughed. Farrah seethed.

"Is there a place for me at this table?" Moose Talbot said, as he came up to Farrah's right with a stacked plate in each hand. Moose used to be in Chad's clique, well, more of a hanger-on. He was a lineman on the football team. Chad and the others were more annoyed with the vulgar brute than anything else, and had started distancing themselves from him.

Bryan looked to his left and right. "I guess not," he quipped as he bit down on a celery stick.

"Fuck you guys," Moose replied. "I don't wanna hang around you anyway. Chandler, everyone knows you're just a homo. And I can't believe you're buddies with this little bitch." He pointed at Donovan.

Jermaine couldn't hear the conversation that was going on at the table, but he heard the word "homo" and read the body language. He had never cared for Moose Talbot. The boy was dangerous. He started to get up—then sat back down. He wanted to see how this played out a little longer, before having to intervene.

"I see you're making a lot of friends, Donovan," Chad said as he tilted back in his chair.

"Yeah," Bryan followed up. "And now he's one of us. And when you jump on one of us, you jump on all of us." Bryan's eyes laid into Moose's.

Moose suddenly lost his nerve. He was pretty sure he could take Chad in a fight. He wasn't so sure about Bryan.

Farrah came in for the save: "Heather, Moose, let's go find a table and get away from the losers' section."

"Aww," Molly said with a sarcastic curl of her lip. "That breaks my heart." Molly Hay and Farrah LaCroix had a rivalry that went back several years. Farrah gave her the one-finger salute as she turned and walked away.

A few minutes later, as Lisa and Donovan were walking out of the gym, his gaze met Jermaine's.

The mentor gave him a broad smile and winked.

The pupil winked back.

17

onovan and Lisa arrived at West Pier at just after ten o'clock. He didn't want to raise the ire of Mike Bailey by bringing his daughter home too late. He figured they had about an hour together.

The two changed into T-shirts and sweatpants in the pavilion, and laid out a blanket under the pavilion's awning. Donovan removed the lemon cake and Mountain Dew from the picnic basket he had prepared earlier that evening. They had the beach to themselves. The night sky was moonless and starless. A gentle breeze caressed them.

"Thanks for taking me to the dance, Donovan. I had a wonderful time. Everything was perfect until Farrah and that ogre came over."

"Yeah. I guess I can now add Moose Talbot to my fans list."

"He's gross. He's just jealous of you, that's all. And Farrah is the meanest girl on Earth. I just don't get her."

"Me neither. I don't think Ted told her that I hurt his arm. He might've been too embarrassed. But one of his friends could have described me to her. She gave me a weird look tonight. I have a feeling things might start to get worse before they get better."

"I just don't get it. You're the sweetest boy I've ever known. Why would anyone want to hurt you? They're just jealous."

Donovan smiled and took a bite of his cake. He adjusted the volume on his cell phone. "Wicked Game" was, not quite accidently, next on the playlist. "You know, Lisa," he started. "Um. We've, uh. We've been dating now for a long time. At least I think we've been dating."

Lisa smiled. "Of course we've been dating."

"Yeah, haha. That's what I thought it was. Anyway…um…I-I just want you to know that I really like you."

"Aww, I really like you too."

While Chris Isaak was expressing his desire to fall in love on the cell phone, Donovan was trying to express his. He swallowed. Took a sip of Mountain Dew. Swallowed again. "I mean, I really, really like you." He fumbled with something in his left pocket. "I guess what I'm trying to say is that I want us to be a couple. Go steady. Whatever it's called." He pulled a small pink box from his pocket and opened it toward Lisa. "Will you be my girlfriend?"

Lisa gazed at the turquoise solitaire with weepy eyes.

"Your birthstone, right?" he asked.

"Yes, but, December has like three different shades of blue. How did you know this was my favorite?"

"I guess I just guessed. It was my favorite too."

"And yes. Yes! I would looove to be your girlfriend."

Donovan, with shaky hands, removed the size six from the box and placed it on the third finger of Lisa's left hand. It fit perfectly.

"I love you, Lisa."

"I love you too, Donovan."

He swept the back of his right hand across her cheek; gently steadied her chin with his thumb and forefinger. And kissed her. His heart pounded. They'd kissed before, sure. Even made out pretty heavily. But this was altogether different. It was official. They were in a committed relationship now.

The next song on the playlist started.

"I noticed that you're a huge Neil Diamond fan," Lisa said with a chuckle.

"Yeah, ha. My grandparents are always listening to the oldies. Motown and stuff. Neil Diamond's my favorite."

A particular lyric got her attention. "What does that mean?"

"The story I heard was that Neil struck out at the club, so he bought a bottle of rose wine on his way home. In the song, he's basically serenading the wine."

"That's weird."

"Yeah. But it's also kinda cool."

They held hands and admired the ring on Lisa's finger. Then they kissed—slowly; softly.

And under that moonless, starless sky, with gentleness, passion, and nervousness, Donovan Marsden and Lisa Bailey lost their virginity to each other.

18

Alec Wilde and Art Mellinger sat across the kitchen table from Reverend Pat and Mrs. Gayle Livingston in their suburban home outside of Valdosta. The four of them were drinking iced sweet tea. Mrs. Livingston was preparing her famous three bean casserole for all of them to enjoy for dinner.

When the visitors arrived, they made small talk and the Livingstons gave them a tour of the house. Pat explained that he was the pastor of a local congregation. It was an independent Baptist church in the Pentecostal tradition, which Alec estimated was just one step above snake handling.

"You folks have a lovely home," Art commented.

"Thankya," Pat said. "The good Lort has provided us well."

"You said on the phone that you men have some questions about Lil Gary and his medication," Gayle said.

Alec nodded. "Yes, ma'am—"

Gayle interrupted, "Is this part of some investigation? Lawsuit? Because that's somethin we'd be intristed in. Just sayin."

Alec and Art briefly looked at each other. "It, ah, may not get to that point ma'am," Art replied. "We're just looking into potential negative side effects of the drug at the moment."

"If it was one of the girls," Pat started, "I wouldn'ta cared. But there was no way I'as havin a boy runt in the family. Lil Gary was 'bout thirteen when the doctor said this drug might help."

"How long did it take before you noticed anything?" Alec asked.

"A few months," Pat replied. "Then the boy sprouted up like grass. Grew a couple inches. T'wasn't long after that, he started gittin weird."

"What happened?" Art asked.

"Lil Gary had always been a sociable boy," Gayle said. "But then he started…to withdraw."

"He wasn't talkin much, 'cept to himself," Pat added. "He was keepin more and more to himself. We got a couple calls from the truancy officer at school. God only knows what he'd been up to. He wouldn't tell us nothin. Said he couldn't r'member."

Pat shifted uneasily in his chair.

"One day—he was spendin a lot of time in the bathroom. So's I knocked on the door to see if he was alright. I says, 'Gary! You okay?' Nothin. So I unlocked the door and walked in; you wouldn't believe what I saw." Pat took a sip of tea. "The boy was sittin on the linoleum facin the commode. His britches were around his ankles. And he was holdin a turd. Turnin it over in his hand like he was studyin it. I says, 'Boy, what in the Lort's name are you doin?' He just looked up at me with this…blank look on 'is face. I swore Satan himself had gotten into 'im."

"It wasn't long after that," Gayle said, "that Trixie, our dog, went missin. Me and Pat just thought she ran away. Then one day—"

Gayle drank from her glass, and Alec and Art noticed that her hands began to shake.

"—I was sweepin in Lil Gary's room and smelt somethin funny near his bed. I got down, pulled up the bedspread, and saw somethin on the floor. I pulled it out. It…it was Trixie. Half rot. On some wax board. Her chest and belly were split open and her skin was pinned down on the wax. Like some sort of dissection—autopsy. Lil Gary said he didn't know anything about it."

"That's when we took 'im to a brain doctor," Pat said.

"A psychiatrist?" Alec asked.

"I s'pose. He said Restor might be to blame for Lil Gary actin strange. We took 'im off it, and almost right away he went back to his ole self."

"His behavior returned to normal?" Art said.

"Yep. It was like he'd never—" The back door slammed shut. "Lil Gary," Pat said. "Come on in here, son."

Lil Gary walked into the kitchen. "Hi, Pa. Ma." He smiled at the two visitors.

Pat said to his son, "These fellers might have some questions for ya."

Gayle removed her casserole from the oven and placed it on the counter to cool.

Art and Alec asked Lil Gary a few questions but didn't get far. After the initial growth spurt, he claimed not to remember anything; as if the entire period was a blackout. Alec had one more question for the teenager.

"Before your memory started to go, do you remember having any physical sensations? Bellyaches? Headaches?"

"I started getting headaches," Lil Gary recalled.

The five of them then finished the conversation and enjoyed Gayle Livingston's three bean casserole.

19

The physician and the research chemist made the short drive back to Art's hotel that evening to discuss what they'd uncovered thus far, if anything. They decided that Alec would spend the night before driving back to Ohio in the morning. As soon as Art closed the door to their room: PHERRRRW!

Alec raised his eyebrows.

"Excuse me," Art said. "I've been holding that in ever since we left."

"Art, Art, blew a fart, blew the whole damn house apart."

"Indeed. And, of course, you know the old saying among people my age: 'Never trust a fart.'"

"That sure was one potent casserole. I can feel some flatulence brewing within me, too."

The duo had stopped to pick up a twelve-pack of Pepsi along the way. Although Art typically enjoyed a cognac or two in the evening, he got the impression that it was better not to drink in front of Alec. He prepared a glass of pop over ice for each of them and they sat at the room's circular table.

"Well, what do we know?" Alec began.

"Spharion A," Art said as he settled in to his seat. "Chemical precursor to the prescription drug Restor. Very effective defoliant. Also very effective as a tissue-rebuilding agent. Used off-label for idiopathic short stature.

"When used 'as indicated' for severe burns, there are no known major side effects.

"When used for ISS, severe side effects are noted in a small portion of the medicated population."

"About how many have been adversely affected?"

"Well over five hundred individuals have been prescribed Restor for ISS. Only six cases have been documented with negative psychological reactions, two of which are unconfirmed regarding the link to the drug. Honestly, if I hadn't witnessed the consequences of it in Vietnam, I wouldn't suspect any link at all."

"And these 'negative psychological reactions' include—?"

"Gradual onset of withdrawal, social isolation, schizophrenic behavior—"

"—Violence and self-harm," Alec added.

"Yeah." Art got up, poured himself another Pepsi, and sat back down.

"Damnit, Alec. There has to be a common denominator; some characteristic they share. If I found it, then this puzzle could be solved."

"You will. We will." Alec took in Art's melancholic expression. "Art, you can't blame yourself."

"I created the damn thing," Art said, in almost a whisper.

"You thought you were doing it for good. There's no way you could have known."

"I suppose." Art exhaled. "That's what I try to tell myself, anyway."

"I guess all of us have our own cross to carry." Alec's face twisted into a sullen look of his own. Art noticed.

"Wanna talk about it?"

Alec got another Pepsi. Sat back down. Tapped the edge of his glass with his wedding band. And began:

"I didn't start college right away. My family was poor and I didn't know what I wanted to do. So for a few years after high school I worked odd jobs, factories, mills. Setting aside money for whatever inspiration would eventually come my way.

"I guess I started drinking pretty heavily towards the tail end of high school. That was pretty much all there was to do in our boring, small town; get drunk on the weekends. After awhile, the weekends led to two or three nights during the week. My parents didn't notice, or if they did, they didn't care.

"Soon after graduation, I moved out on my own. I would always work first-shift and second-shift jobs. I didn't want to work at night. My nights were reserved for getting loaded. *Every* night. Mostly beer for a while, but that gradually morphed into more and more liquor. I had my share of scrapes with the law, but nothing major. I wasn't a social butterfly. I preferred to drink alone, usually in my own home. Pondering my life; pondering the future.

"One night, *Trapper John, M.D.* just happened to be on TV while I was tying one on. I was mesmerized.

And that's when I knew. That's when I knew that I wanted to be a physician.

"I always had to work on the side throughout the academic phase of med school. Student loans helped a lot, but I always had to have a part-time job to make the ends meet. It was sometime during my first year, when I came to an epic realization. I didn't refer to it then as a problem. I referred to it as my *thing.* And in addition to juggling school and work my thing was a need to get drunk every night. Not just drunk, hammered. I told myself that I could continue what I was doing as long as I always obeyed one rule: don't fuck up. So I worked and studied during the day, and drank at night.

"Fast forward several years: I got married, built a private practice, and became an associate doctor with the Cleveland Clinic. The administration at the clinic started noticing some disturbing trends beginning in medicine. Even then, they saw that many prescriptions for opioid pain-killers led to out-of-control addiction. So they started a wellness program; and appointed me to be the chief wellness director. How ironic is that? An alcoholic whose job, in part, is to combat addiction. Anyway. At about that same time, a friend of Emily's who worked as a local CNN-affiliated journalist, jokingly said that I had a 'face for radio.' Ha. That remark led to me making a few appearances on the network as a medical commentator. Life was good. I was kicking ass in my chosen field, and my wife was a hotshot attorney with a major firm, on the brink of making partner. Yep. Life was good. And then one night—"

Alec arose from his seat, walked over to the mini-bar, and took three gulps of a new can of Pepsi. He then poured the rest into his glass. After releasing a loud belch, he returned to the table.

"And then one night, I was at home finishing up my third double scotch and water. I got a call from one of the interns at a clinic facility where I made rounds. A mother had brought in her little girl, five years old, who had slurred speech and loss of coordination of about a few days' duration. The intern didn't know how to proceed. He pleaded with me to come in and take a look. Even though I told him that I wasn't on-call, he practically begged me to come anyway. Against my better judgment, I agreed.

"I performed an exam, and given the unremarkable history, I figured she was likely suffering from ischemia, perhaps due to a congenital heart defect. I made arrangements to have her transferred to a center that was better equipped to handle such cases. And that was it. I went home.

"The girl died three hours later.

"The family initiated a malpractice suit. It turned out that the little girl didn't have ischemia. It was a cerebral hemorrhage. A simple CT scan at my facility would have confirmed that. So, her attorney claimed I was negligent.

"During the discovery process, it was revealed that the little girl and her mother were in a severe auto accident while she was doped up on heroin, a week before the girl's death. The mother chose not to disclose that to me when I met her. Had I known that, obviously, I would have ordered the scan.

"So, I was exonerated of that. What I wasn't exonerated of—was being under the influence.

"The intern and several others at the facility testified that they smelled alcohol on my breath that night. I was honest about it. The fallout...

"It was a pretty big deal in the local news. My license was suspended for a year. The Cleveland Clinic asked me to resign my position. CNN stopped contacting me for my medical opinions on their news programs. And my wife...well, my wife was forced out of her law firm. We decided to start over in Harbor Light. And it's been pretty rough-going ever since."

A moment of silence elapsed. Art broke it.

"Well, from what I know of you, you'll turn it around. You'll have happy days again."

"I hope." Alec stood up and arched his back. AAAAARNT! "Damn, those beans were magnificent going in; not so much coming out."

Art leaned over in his chair. PHERRRW! "I better check myself after that one," he said. The two doubled-over with laughter.

"Why are farts so funny?" Alec asked. "We probably have sixteen years of college education between us, and here we are laughing like school-boys."

"Let's never grow up, Alec!"

"Absolutely!"

Later, the two turned off the lights and retired to their twin beds. Just before sleep overcame them, Alec said,

"Rose."

"Excuse me?"

"The little girl. Her name was Rose."

Then they slept.

20

October 9, 2018

Donovan Marsden awoke with a headache.

PART THREE

DECLINE

1

It was a windy, chilly Tuesday morning, the sixteenth of October. Fall had surely made its presence known.

Farrah LaCroix was wondering how it was even possible for that little shit to have bested her new part-time lover in a fight. Finally, after much cajoling, she was able to get Ted to admit how his arm had gotten fucked up. Sitting in English Lit., her mind wasn't on Shakespeare. It was on revenge.

Jermaine Barrison was thinking that the incoming freshmen in his gym class continued to be fatter year after year. He liked to believe that introducing the kids to exercise and good dietary habits had a positive impact, but if this national obesity epidemic wasn't dealt with seriously, then it would only get worse.

Chad Chandler was thinking about whether he could keep his secret (which was already somewhat of a rumor) safe for the rest of the school year. After graduation, he would be *free*; free to live his life as he saw fit; beyond the false persona created by his family and friends. He would be able to do that *then*; not *now*. No matter how hip and open-minded high school living had become, it could still be a cruel and immature prison. No, he'd ride out the rest of the year with that little tidbit kept under his hat.

Donovan Marsden was thinking how he needed to keep it together during his encounter with Dr. Wilde in a few minutes. At the last appointment, Dr. Wilde had said he wanted to alter the appointment schedule from bi-monthly to monthly, "just to be safe."

There was no way he could tell the doctor about the things that had started about a week ago. No way in heck! The headaches at first would kind of come and go, but they were becoming more frequent. Not long after his first headache, he'd started getting a ringing in his ears, again intermittent, and again more frequent. And what was up with his concentration lately? Donovan had always had a keen attention span, one of the reasons why his grades were so good. But, he'd noticed during the last few days that his mind would wander quite a bit. Yesterday, he'd barely finished his calculus test on time.

I can't tell Dr. Wilde about any of this, he thought. He had come too far. Just a few months ago he had been nothing; worthless. Just an ugly, puny kid who got laughed at and bullied. Got the crap kicked out of him. Now. Now it was completely different. He was handsome and well-liked. He had popular friends and a pretty girlfriend. And he had something else he'd never had before: respect. Both self-respect and that of others. These *things*, what Dr. Wilde would call symptoms, were probably just temporary any way. Everyone got headaches sometimes, right? They were worth putting up with for a while in order to keep the life he now had. He knew that Restor was mainly responsible for his transformation from nobody to somebody—and he wasn't giving it up. *I'm not giving it up!*

"Donovan...the doctor will see you now."

2

general appearance: unremarkable
"How's school?"

"Eh. It's okay." Donovan sat on the exam table, trying to keep an even tone and level head.

"Step on up to the scale."

height: 5'2 and three-fourths

weight: 132 lbs

"Whatever happened with that girl you were kind of sweet on? What's her name—?"

"Lisa."

"Yeah. How'd it go?"

"Great. She's my girlfriend now."

"Aww. Good for you."

heart/lung auscultation: unremarkable

Alec attached a cuff to Donovan's left arm. "Open up," he said, and placed a thermometer in his mouth. "Think the football team will make it to the playoffs?"

Donovan shrugged.

"They sure are good this year."

blood pressure: 130/84

pulse: 88

temperature: 100.7

respiration: 16

"Let me know if any of this hurts."

abdominal palpation: hypertonicity; all quadrants. (likely due to exercise)

"I'd be surprised if you weren't having any growing pains. Any back or other joint pain?"

"Eh. Just a little achiness sometimes in my back." Donovan played along.

"Headaches?"

"Nope," Donovan lied.

"Well, all of your vitals are a little up from your last exam, but the one that really concerns me is your temperature. It looks like you're running a fever."

No, no, no! I can't blow this. I can't throw it all away because of a crummy fever! Donovan thought fast and winged it.

"Oh. I forgot. I've been coughing a little the last couple of days, and I had a bit of a runny nose yesterday. Could that explain it?"

Donovan and Dr. Wilde eyed each other without expression for a few seconds.

"You bet. It could even explain the increase in some of your other vitals. The common cold is much more common whenever the season changes. It certainly has gotten cooler lately. Let us know if your cold symptoms don't ease up over the next few days, and I'll write you something. Otherwise...I guess we're good to go for another month."

Good to go...thank God! Donovan exhaled and smiled appreciatively.

3

University of Texas, Austin
Lyndon Baines Johnson Hall
March 20, 1978

"Three days into spring break and I'm already bored to death."

"Yeah, a couple of wild ones we are."

"I think I'll just stay here and sleep the rest of the week away. Hey, Braxton, what do you want to do when you finally get out of this place?"

"I don't know."

"No, really, Jeremy. What do you want to do after it's all said and done?"

"I don't know, B.J. I just don't know. I never asked you— what does B.J. stand for?"

"Bartlett Joshua."

"That's modern."

"Blame my father, and his father before him. At least it doesn't stand for Blow Job."

"That's right; I forgot. You're B.J. Wentworth *the third*."

"What's your major again?"

"Finance."

"What the hell are you going to do with that?"

"For the umpteenth time, I don't know!"

"You know what?"

"What?"

"Pig's butt."

"Nice."

"I have an idea."

"Miracles do happen."

"No, really, Jeremy. Hear me out. I majored in pharmacology because my pharmacist dad thought it would be cool for us to work together. But, I just don't see myself working as a pharmacist in some small drugstore for the rest of my life. I wanna go big, man. And do you know where big is?"

"I'm all ears."

"Pharmaceutical companies. Man, it's the wave of the future. They're makin a ton of dough, and the market will never go down because pretty much everyone has at least one prescription that their doctors say they need. That's where the action is."

"And sooo...?"

"And so we should start a drug company."

"Huh?"

"Look, your family's sittin on a boat-load of money. Your dad would invest if we gave him a good pitch. With your resources and business background, and my knowledge of the pharmaceutical industry, we'd make out like bandits."

"I don't know. It sounds a little far-fetched."

"But it isn't, though! We start out small and work our way up. We can call it Wentworth-Braxton."

"Braxton-Wentworth sounds better."

"Yes! Yes, it does! Braxton-Wentworth, baby."

"Tell ya what. Bring it up again when we get closer to graduation, which seems like a million years away. I have to admit, you got me curious."

"Attaboy."

4

Tiffany McIntosh had had better mornings. Her boyfriend Brad, who she absolutely adored, had dumped her a few weeks ago. She was still struggling with the separation. To make matters worse, she was a week late on her period. Due to running out of gas, she was also late to her job today at Marriott North in Las Vegas. *Some girls never get a break,* she thought, as she cleaned countertops in the cafe. The breakfast crowd was heavy, yet the tips sucked. Just another wonderful day in her life.

Tiffany was putting away some cleaning supplies in the back office when her boss said, "I need you to deliver this to the guest on the patio." He handed her a twice-folded piece of paper.

"What is it?"

"Beats me. Someone just dropped it off at the front desk and asked that it be given to the man in the suit on the patio."

She took the piece of paper and, as she made her way towards the sliding glass door, noticed that there was in fact a man in a suit on the patio. The only guest on the patio. He was wearing a dark blue sport coat and slacks, with a white shirt and red tie, lounging on a chair and reading a magazine. Even though he was wearing sunglasses, Tiffany guessed that he was Asian. (Is it Asian or oriental? Oh, wait. She'd learned in junior college last year that *people* are Asian; *things* are oriental. Got it.)

He looked like an important person, so this must be an important note. Before walking through the door and delivering it to the man in the suit, Tiffany couldn't help but sneak a peek at the note. It consisted of three typed lines:

Arthur Mellinger
103 Walnut St.
Racine, Wisconsin

5

Donovan came home from school and immediately went to bed. He wanted to escape his nagging headache for a couple hours. He had the house to himself and decided to take advantage of the peace and quiet, so he plopped down on the lower bunk in his room, stretched, and closed his eyes.

Donovan was standing in the middle of a field of lilies. A sea of white, as far as the eye could see.

Coach Barrison was standing to his left about fifty yards away, looking at him with an ear-to-ear smile. Jermaine was wearing his typical attire, a Polo-style shirt and coach's shorts.

Standing to Jermaine's left, an equal distance away, was Chad Chandler. Chad was wearing his football uniform, but in lieu of his helmet, he wore his homecoming crown. He had an even expression on his face.

Knock knock knock

Standing to Chad's left was Lisa Bailey. She gazed at Donovan with a deep frown. An old, charcoal-colored barn was behind her. She looked sad; hurt; afraid. What's wrong, Lisa? he tried to say, but couldn't. She started to turn...towards the barn. She can't go in there, *Donovan thought.* No. No!

Knock knock knock

Is someone at the door? Cripe, he'd barely gotten a wink of sleep. And what was that dream about? Donovan lumbered out of bed and made his way down the hall. *Maybe it's just a salesman.* He opened the door and Rodney was standing there, holding a G.I. Joe jeep with two action figures in the front seats in his hand.

"Hey," Rodney said.

"Hey."

Rodney waited for Donovan to invite him in. When it didn't happen, "I thought I'd give this stuff back. You left it at my house the last time you were over."

"That must have been...what...two months ago." Donovan regretted the words as soon as they escaped his mouth.

"Yeah." The two dropped their heads for a moment. Rodney broke the silence. "Dude, what's going on? I never see you. You don't even talk to me on Facebook anymore."

"I don't know, Rodney. It's...it's just that...I've been spending a lot of time with Lisa—"

"And the guys."

"Yeah. And the guys."

Rodney's eyes welled. "Dude...we were always best friends. Geek squad to the end."

Donovan open his mouth to say something, but the words weren't there.

"It's like you traded me for something better."

Donovan noticed a burning anger rising in his own chest, and tried to quell it.

"You traded your old life for a better new life. It's like I don't matter anymore—"

"You have no idea!" Donovan snapped. He stepped through the doorway, allowing the door to slam shut behind him, and joined Rodney on the porch, just inches from him. "I was nothing! People picked on me, or laughed at me, or ignored me."

"Dude, in case you didn't notice, I got picked on, laughed at, and ignored too. Still do."

Donovan got ahold of himself. "Look…Rodney. It's just…it's just that I really love my life now." (Headaches, tinnitus, and attention deficits aside.) "I really love my life…and…and—"

"And you have no time for me."

"That's not it." Donovan thought for a moment. "Hey, when the football season's over, I'll have more time for us to hang out. It'll be like before. You'll see."

"Okay," Rodney said, but both of them knew it wasn't true. "Here's your stuff. Guess I'll…see ya around."

"See ya around."

Donovan closed the door and considered the conversation he'd just had. He missed Rodney, but he certainly didn't miss his former existence. And he realized that his close lifelong bond with Rodney was likely a thing of the past.

6

After several weeks of being apart, Alec Wilde figured it was time that he and his wife Emily had *the talk*. He had phoned her earlier that day, and was now on his way to their home *(Will it continue to be our home?)* with Italian take-out for dinner.

He didn't know what to expect. In fact, he had no expectations at all. But he packed a travel bag just in case.

They made polite small talk during the meal, then settled into the living room with coffee. She sat at one end of their large, beige couch, he at the other.

"I've been doing a lot of thinking," he said.

"Me too."

He smiled. "I really miss our early days."

"I do, too," Emily said, returning the smile. "We were just a couple of kids in love, living on hot dogs and Ramen noodles and our dreams."

"You didn't have to live on hot dogs and Ramen noodles," Alec reminded her. "You did that for my sake."

"I suppose. But I wouldn't have traded it for the world."

"Remember that crazy ferret we had?"

"It kept pooping on the carpet!"

They laughed.

She inched closer to the middle of the couch.

"I don't know what happened to us, Em. Somewhere, on our way up, I think we just...I don't know."

"Lost sight of us. Lost sight of what brought us together. Lost sight of our love; our marriage. And when we had to start over—"

Now it was Alec who moved closer to the middle.

"—We didn't know what to do," he finished for her.

"I almost hated you for it. I blamed everything on you, whether you deserved it or not."

"I deserved it."

"Alec, I don't have a sensible explanation for why I cheated on you. Maybe it was my way of trying to escape the bitterness I had for you. But, I'm sorry. I wish I could take it all back. I'm so, so sorry."

Alec placed his arm on the back of the couch and began playing with her black hair between his thumb and forefinger.

"But, if you give us another chance," she continued, "I'll do everything I can to make it work. I realized when you were gone that you're the best thing that ever happened to me. I don't ever want to lose you."

She placed her arm on top of his.

"I'm sorry too, Em. I'm sorry for putting us in this position. All I can do is work at being a better person each day...every day...with you." He smiled and winked.

"Let's go to bed," she said.

Alec fetched his travel bag.

7

Diary entry of Donovan Marsden
dated October 18, 2018

We have a good chance at beating Vermilion tomorrow. It's an away game, but I don't think I'll be going. I haven't been feeling very sociable lately. I had an interesting conversation with Chad today after school. Without coming right out and saying it, he basically told me that he's gay. I guess I wasn't surprised. It must be hard for him though, to keep it a secret. Chad seems so perfect, I didn't think he had any problems. He said he can't wait to graduate and get out of high school. That's the funny thing. He can't wait to get out of school and I'm just starting to like it. I wouldn't have seen that coming a few months ago. We have a good chance at beating Vermilion tomorrow. Damn. I cut my thumb in art class today. It hurts like a bitch. Lisa and I have been arguing a lot. I don't know why. I guess it's my fault. I'm always so distracted and easily annoyed. We had a spat today. I forget what it was about. I'll apologize to her. I don't want to lose her. We have a good chance at beating Vermilion tomorrow. Well, I guess it's time to go to bed. Goodnight.

8

Alec and Emily Wilde were at home watching *The Magnificent Seven* for what seemed like the thousandth time. They had first seen the movie while they were dating, at a dollar matinee. That was when they'd first had the debate: who was cooler, Yul Brynner or Steve McQueen? Emily had voted McQueen. Alec, Brynner.

Alec checked his phone during a break to make more popcorn. There was a missed call and message from a now-familiar number: "Alec, it's Art. Give me a call back as soon as you get this. *It's important.*" The urgency in Art's voice was unmistakable.

Alec told Emily to unpause the movie without him. He had to make a personal call. Sitting alone at the kitchen table, he called his friend back.

"Alec."

"Art, what's going on?"

"I found it, Alec. The common denominator. It took a lot of digging, but I've finally uncovered it."

"The link?" Alec asked. "The thing that links all of Restor's bad effects together? What is it?" He felt his heart pounding in his chest.

"Several cases have the same trait. I even recently contacted several old acquaintances from Vietnam who confirmed the same situation, back when Spharion A was used. Oh, and remember the good Reverend Livingston? It turns out he wasn't always preaching the Word of God. He did jail time for persistent disorderly conduct."

Alec was getting restless. "What *is* it?"

"A parental history of psychopathy."

Joe Marsden.

Among the Marsden household, Alec had Nancy, Donovan, and Mikey as patients, but not Joe. He did not regard this as entirely unusual. Sometimes, one or both parents prefer seeing another primary care physician for their health needs, other than the one who cares for the rest of the family.

Alec knew nothing about Joe's medical history, apart from bits in Donovan's and Mikey's files in terms of heredity. He also knew he had to speak with Joe as soon as possible. The chances of Joe being psychopathic were virtually nil, but Alec had to rule it out for Donovan's sake, and, in no small part, for his own peace of mind. He decided he would call Joe in the morning.

Art said that he would tie up his findings and compile a report that he'd present to the government. He promised that he'd be in touch with Alec soon.

Upon disconnecting the call, Alec thought about Art Mellinger. He pondered their relationship. The two had become fast friends while working on a mystery.

He had bared his soul to Art regarding his past and his marriage, which he'd found to be immensely therapeutic.

He very much liked Art. He looked forward to talking with him again soon.

9

*I*nstead of lilies, they were now standing among dandelions; an endless carpet of yellow.

Coach Barrison still displayed his broad grin, but his formerly pearly white teeth were now a dark brown; jagged and corroded.

A maggot crawled out of the corner of his mouth.

Another.

Then a huge ball of maggots dropped from his head as his jaw fell away.

As before, Chad was standing to Coach's left. He was still wearing his football uniform, but not his crown. In its place was a ballcap that read Queer and Proud! *He still had the even countenance on his face. Occupying the orbits where his chestnut eyes should have been were two giant beetles, moving around in clumsy circles.*

Lisa continued walking towards the old barn.

No! Lisa, don't! *Again, Donovan mouthed the words but could not hear them.*

She turned to look at him. Tears were streaming down both of her cheeks.

I'm sorry, honey! Don't go in there! I love you! I love you!

She slowly turned away, and disappeared into the barn.

10

The first thing that Alec Wilde did when he arrived to his office on Friday the nineteenth was call Joe Marsden at his job. He didn't quite know how to lure Joe into a conversation, so he simply said that he'd like to discuss Donovan's medication with him. Joe agreed to stop over during his lunch hour.

Alec was studying Donovan's file when he heard a knock at the door.

"Mr. Marsden is here to see you," Melanie said.

Joe walked in and extended his hand to Alec. "Hey, Doc. What's on your mind?"

"Hi Joe. Good to see you. Please, have a seat." Joe sat in one of two chairs in front of Alec's desk. Alec wondered where to begin.

"I hope everything's okay," Joe said.

"Oh, sure. Sure. There's just, uh. Well, I spoke with someone in the pharmaceutical industry. He informed me that there are potentially serious side effects with Restor; with patients who have a family history of mental health illness."

Joe crossed his legs and folded his arms across his abdomen, as if protecting himself.

"I just want to rule that out in Donovan's case," Alec said. "I know you're not under my care. Do you have a primary care doctor?"

"Yeah, I see a guy in Avon."

"Oh. What's his name? Maybe I know him."

"Eh, his name escapes me at the moment," Joe lied.

"Well. Is there anything I should be concerned about? Any mental health topics?" Alec realized that he probably sounded ridiculous to Joe.

"No, I can't say I'm crazy or anything. Although Nancy would probably disagree."

They laughed.

"I also wanted to ask you about Donovan, Joe. The last time he was in, he said he wasn't experiencing any bad sensations or effects from his medication. It's not uncommon for a patient not to be entirely truthful about side effects if they really don't want to give the drug up. Have you noticed any abnormal behaviors in Donovan at home?"

"No. Not at all," Joe lied again.

Joe felt relieved as he left Dr. Wilde's office building. As if he could breathe. He'd felt like he was suffocating during their meeting.

So what if Donovan was acting a little weird lately? *He's a teenager. Teenagers are weird.*

The changes in Donovan were nothing short of miraculous. And Restor was the reason. Restor and that Coach Barrison. Joe was as excited as his boy about Donovan's transformation. Probably more so. No son of Joseph Lexington Marsden was going to be a puny little nerd. Donovan would remain on Restor as long as it took. If there were a few hiccups along the road, then so be it. *What's the term? Collateral damage.* There was probably no connection between Restor and Joe's condition anyway.

And what of that?

Joe had realized decades ago that his life was shit. Years of bar fights, misdemeanors, and getting fired from dead-end jobs had gotten him no where. He could have offed himself, sure. But why should he have? Why should he have let the pissants and whores have the last laugh? His life sucked, not because he was beneath people, quite the opposite. He was better than everyone. That was why he was having such a hard time of it. He figured that if he was going to remain in this shitstain world, then he better try to bring himself down and fit in with the underlings.

So he had gone to see a doctor who'd referred him to another doctor. And that doctor had almost immediately diagnosed him with psychopathy. Psychopathy? As in psycho? He was no psycho, he'd thought at the time. Everyone else was just dumb.

But, he played along. He took medication to help calm his temper and supposed delusions. He attended both private and group therapy sessions. He even eased up on his beloved Natty Light. He met Nancy and got a steady, entry-level gig at Midwest Mowers, where he worked his way up to middle management. *Although I should be president of the company.* His doctor visits and therapy sessions weren't conducted in Avon, but farther north in Mentor. *I can't let anyone in the vicinity of Harbor Light know about this.* Only Nancy knew of his treatments. He still loathed living in a world of inferiors, but he was getting along. Coping.

He wouldn't tell Nancy (or anyone else for that matter) about his little talk with Dr. Wilde. *There's nothing to worry about. Nothing at all.*

11

Lisa accompanied her boyfriend to the locker room after school. Donovan decided that he would do some chores here so the team would have fresh towels and clean water bottles when they met in a couple hours for their away game at Vermilion. He wouldn't be going. Nor did he feel like spending time with Lisa. He just wanted to go home and be by himself.

"I don't understand why you've been so distant," she said.

"Huh?"

"It's like you're not with it sometimes."

Donovan poured some detergent into the washer and began filling it with linens.

"And I can't believe how much you're swearing," she followed up.

"Like you never swear."

"Not nearly as much as you."

He turned the washer on, then squirted some dish soap into one of two adjoining basins.

"Why can't you tell me what is wrong with y—"

"Why can't you get the hell off my back?" he said, more loudly than he'd intended.

"You can be such a jerk sometimes!" Lisa said as she stormed out of the room.

Way to go, Marsden, he thought. *You handled that one well. Boyfriend of the Year.*

He started filling one of the basins with cold water. *I'll apologize to her later. She's right, though. I can certainly be a jerk sometimes; even though I don't mean to be.*

He turned the faucet to the other tub and ran hot water in it. Then he dumped the water bottles to be cleaned into it. *I'll apologize and everything will be okay—*

"Y'know, ever hear that payback's a bitch?"

Donovan recognized the voice instantly.

Here we go again.

He turned around, and there they were, lined-up: Ted Mullins, Farrah LaCroix, Moose Talbot, and Chucky Vasquez.

"Another unlucky day for you, my friend. And no one's here to save your sorry ass," Chucky said as he stepped forward. Donovan couldn't help notice the improvement in Chucky's articulation. Last summer's speech therapy had gone well.

Donovan noticed something else as well. Unlike his previous run-ins, he wasn't scared. Or angry. He wasn't even nervous.

Without warning, Chucky launched a roundhouse kick with his right leg, hoping to cave in Donovan's side.

Donovan caught the lower leg in his left armpit. Then he threw his left leg over Chucky's and the two fell to the floor.

Donovan crossed his own feet, trapping Chucky's entire lower extremity. With Chucky's foot still clutched in his underarm, Donovan grasped his left forearm with his right hand.

And torqued.

Chucky's ankle snapped.

"HOLY SHIIIT!"

Ted swiftly moved over and kicked Donovan in the back of the head. Twice.

"Damnit, don't mark his face!" Farrah screamed. She had long ago learned not to leave obvious visible damage while administering beatings to her victims.

"Fuck, where'd he learn to fight like that?" Ted asked.

"Coach Barrison," came Moose's reply. "I saw 'em training in the gym."

Disoriented from the blows to his head, Donovan was unable to fight off Ted and Chucky as they held him down on his belly, per Farrah's instructions.

She undid Donovan's pants button and zipper, and in one savage motion, jerked his jeans and underwear to his knees.

There was a broom in the corner.

"Moose, hold his legs," Farrah said.

Moose hesitated. "Hey, maybe this is a little heavy. I don't wanna get in trouble."

Farrah snarled. "Shut up and do what you're told, fatass!" He shut up and did what he was told.

She fetched the broom and casually walked back. "This is going to hurt you a lot more than me," she said.

Farrah shoved the broom handle into Donovan's rectum.

—*Sitting on his bedroom floor with Mikey, throwing paper wads for Butterscotch to bat around. Mikey laughing deliriously. Donovan always loved it when his little brother laughed like that.*

—*Sitting across from Lisa in a booth at Burger King. Each sipping on a milkshake. Staring into each other's eyes. Smiling. Wordlessly.*

—*Playing G.I. Joe with Rodney. Duke (Rodney's main action figure) and Flint (Donovan's) are about to break into Cobra headquarters and take down Cobra Commander and Destro.*

—*Fishing with Chad Chandler. Donovan's reeling in a huge walleye.*

—*Lifting weights with Jermaine. Coach is teaching him how to properly perform bicep curls with dumbbells.* "Exhale on the positive. Inhale on the negative. Concentrate on squeezing the muscle. Keep the movement very smooth. Very controlled."

—*The dandelion field had turned white. Everywhere a thick cloud of dandelion spores blowing. The old barn is still there; barely visible. No sign of Jermaine, Chad, and Lisa. They're gone. I'm all alone…all alone…all alone…*

Donovan was in fact all alone when he started to regain consciousness. He heard fading voices in the distance:

"I hope we don't get in trouble."

"We're not going to get in trouble."

"Yeah, y'know, it's not like he's gonna tell anyone."

12

Six days elapsed.

13

Thursday

Donovan hadn't been to school all week. He'd told his parents last weekend that he was coming down with symptoms of the flu: fever, headaches, joint pain. *Maybe that's what all this is. It's the beginning of flu season anyway, right? Yeah. The flu.* A few more days and all this would go away. He'd be good as new. Although the flu didn't explain his lack of concentration and fucked-up thoughts. That's what was going through his mind as he lay in bed this morning.

Friday after the attack, he was able to stagger to his car and drive home. He knew he should have driven to the local ER (it had taken a day for his rectum to stop bleeding), but there was no way he could have done that. The shame; the embarrassment; and everyone would find out. No. No one would ever find out. The Cunt of the Century, Farrah LaCroix, and her Merry Band of Bastards wouldn't risk incriminating themselves by telling anyone either. *Just put it out of your mind, Donovan*, he thought. *It never happened.*

He crawled out of bed and made his way toward the kitchen. Although he hadn't had much of an appetite at all this week, he decided that he would force himself to eat something. Don't want to lose any of that hard-earned muscle by starving. Speaking of hard-earned muscle, it had been over a week since he'd last worked out. Oh well. He'd been hitting the weights non-stop for months. A week or two off might do his body some good.

Donovan took his power breakfast (three scrambled eggs with shredded cheese and a glass of orange juice) outside on the porch, and had a seat on the top step. It was a crisp, yet sunny morning. As he began eating, a rabbit appeared out of the bushes, chewing on the lawn.

"Good morning, Mr. Rabbit," Donovan said. "How's the grub?"

"Good morning, young sir," Mr. Rabbit said. "Fine, just fine. How are you?"

"Okay, I guess. Considering."

The rabbit looked away, then back at Donovan. "Say, you haven't seen Mr. Fox around, have you?" it asked.

"I don't know if I've ever seen foxes around here," Donovan replied.

"Oh, they're around alright. Yes, yes. And they often hunt in packs; preying on innocent little creatures like me. I suppose you may know something about that; being preyed upon."

"Yeah. I suppose."

"Just remember, young sir. As long as you are a rabbit, you'll always be hunted by foxes. Do you understand?"

"I think so."

"Good. I must be going. Take care, my friend."

"Take care, Mr. Rabbit." Donovan took one last bite of cheesy eggs and washed it down with two chugs of OJ.

Jermaine Barrison was wrapping up today's first-period gym class. He settled into his small office with a cup of coffee, thinking.

It was his weekend to have his ten-year-old son, Jamal. Jamal has an affinity for scary movies, so Jermaine figured that he would take his boy to HalloWeekends at Cedar Point amusement park this Saturday. Jamal would love the haunted houses. His dad would, too. Something else was on Jermaine's mind.

Once again this week, Donovan Marsden had been absent from class. Donovan, his student; acolyte; *friend*.

Donovan hadn't been right for a couple weeks. And it wasn't any one thing. It was several. During gym; while exercising; helping out in the weight room—Donovan seemed—*off*. Distracted. A few times he'd caught Donovan talking to himself. Jermaine hadn't thought anything of it, but now, looking back, he'd never noticed the youngster doing that before. It wasn't like Donovan to miss school or his training sessions, and it had been over a week since they had worked out together. Something was wrong. Maybe he'd arrange a meeting with Principal Winter to discuss it.

Racine Journal Times—Obituaries—Thursday,
October 25, 2018
Arthur Stanley Mellinger, PhD.
November 19, 1943—October 23, 2018

RACINE—Arthur S. Mellinger passed away suddenly on Tuesday at his home in Racine…

Diary entry of Donovan Marsden
dated October 25, 2018

Lisa broke up with me. Did it while texting. Can't say I blame her. It hurts. It huuuurts. Tonight's dinner was good. Macaroni and cheese. I'll get her back. Yeah. I'll make up to her. It'll be okay. Yeah. Like it was. My head hurts so fucking bad. I can't concentrate. Mikey keeps asking what's wrong with me. The flu. Yeah. The flu. We play Clyde tomorrow. Home game. Don't think I'll make it. I told Mikey I'll feel better in a few days. I'll make it up to Lisa. Rodney too. It'll be like before. Yeah. I think I'll shut my phone off now. Not in the mood to talk to anyone. Anymore. I think I'll play with Butterscotch. Playee with Butterscotch. PLAYEEEE with Butterscotch. I have a feeling I have a feeling I have tomorrow's going to suck. How much worse can it get, huh? Goodbye.

Part Four

The Occurrence in Harbor Light

1

Friday, October 26, 2018

8:27 a.m.

Jermaine Barrison arrived at Principal Doug Winter's office a few minutes ahead of his appointment. He was leafing through an old edition of *Sports Illustrated* when the secretary waved him in.

"Jermaine, good morning," Doug said. "Please, have a seat." They shook hands. "What would you like to discuss?"

"Doug, it's about Donovan Marsden," Jermaine replied.

"Oh, yes, Donovan. It's amazing what you've done with that boy. I'm sure he really looks up to you."

"Well, the admiration is mutual. Which is why I'm here."

"Oh?"

"Doug...Donovan hasn't been himself over the last couple three weeks. He can't seem to concentrate, he's missed training sessions, which he never does, and he's been out of school all week—"

"Yes, his mother says he has the flu. She's been picking up his assignments after school."

Jermaine hesitated. "I think there may be something else going on. Something deeper than the flu."

"What do you think?"

"I'm not sure, but it might be related to that medication he's on. I don't know what it's called, but I think we should touch base with his doctor. I'm sure the physician information would be in Donovan's file."

"Don't you think that if Donovan was experiencing any negative side effects, he or his parents would have already informed his doctor?"

Jermaine leaned forward in his chair.

"Doug, I've seen that boy progress with a gleam in his eye that I've never seen before. He is so proud of how far he's come and where he is now. He'll do anything he can in order to stay on that medication. The last thing he'd do would be to alarm his physician and give him reason to pull the drug."

Principal Winter considered this for a moment.

"Jermaine, it would be highly inappropriate, if not illegal, for us to directly contact his physician instead of the parents." Doug tapped his finger on his desk a few times. "I'll tell you what, maybe I'll stick around a bit today after school and have a word with Mrs. Marsden when she comes in to pick up Donovan's assignments."

"Okay," Jermaine said. "But I doubt it'll help. From what I gather, his father is even more excited about him being on that drug than Donovan."

Lisa Bailey and Rodney McAllister sat at the same table in the library during second-period study hall. After a prolonged silence, Rodney piped up:

"How's Donovan?"

"I guess I don't know," Lisa said. "We broke up a couple days ago."

"What?" he heard himself say, a little too loudly.

"Shhhhh!" from the librarian.

"Dude, what happened?"

"I'm not a dude. I'm a dudette."

"Duly noted. It just seemed like you guys were the perfect couple."

"I don't know, Rodney. I love him, but he's been so mean and out of it lately. I don't know what's going on. He won't talk to me."

"I haven't seen him in school all week."

"The last time we texted, he said he had the flu."

"Are you doing anything after school?"

"No. Why?"

"We should stop over to see Donovan for a surprise visit. Maybe that'll cheer him up. Maybe we can help break him from whatever spell he's under."

"Okay."

12:08 p.m.

Maureen Adams, Principal Winter's secretary, looked up from her Subway sandwich and was surprised to see Jermaine Barrison in the administration's quarters for the second time today.

"Hi, Mr. Barrison. Can I help you?"

"Hi, Maureen. I'm sorry to bother you during lunch, but I think I left my phone in Mr. Winter's office. Is it okay if I go in and check?"

Maureen frowned slightly. Doug Winter was fairly stern when he instructed his staff not to allow anyone in his office while he was away. But certainly this was an exception. Mr. Barrison was just looking for his phone. No potential harm in that.

"Sure," she said. She fished in her desk drawer for the key and let Jermaine into the dark room...and waited for him at the door.

Jermaine turned his head toward her and said, "I'll just be a sec, Maureen. I'll lock up when I'm done."

Hesitating briefly, she replied, "Okay. Sure. Take your time," and went back to her desk.

Jermaine wondered where the student files were kept as he looked around at the plethora of filing cabinets. *Has to be here somewhere,* he thought. After opening a few to no avail and spending what seemed like an hour, he finally found the right cabinet.

"M, M, where are the Ms?" he whispered. He opened one drawer. Then another. At last, he pulled a file labeled: MARSDEN, DONOVAN.

"Mr. Barrison?" he heard Maureen's voice call.

Getting caught combing through student files would earn him a firm reprimand at best, and outright termination at worst. He had to be quick.

Upon opening the file, he took a glance and a few words struck out:

Idiopathic Short Stature.

Restor.

Dr. Alec Wilde.

"Mr. Barrison?" A shadow was approaching.

Jermaine swiftly replaced the file and gently slid the drawer closed producing a barely-audible *click.*

"Mr. Barrison." The lights in the room turned on.

"Oh, hey, Maureen. I guess it isn't here after all. I looked everywhere."

"Well, I'm sure you would have found it by now if it was. Maybe you left it in your office, or one of the restrooms."

"Yeah, maybe. I'll check. Thanks Maureen."

2:46 p.m.

Rodney and Lisa both missed the bus and made the short walk to the Marsden residence. Rodney knocked on the door and it was almost instantly opened.

"Hi, Rodney! Hi, Lisa!" said little Mikey Marsden.

"Hey, buddy," Rodney said. "Is your big brother home? We came over to check on him."

"Nooo. I don't know where he is. He was s'posed to be here to look after me."

Lisa peered into the house. "Mikey, are you here alone?"

"Yeah, but I ain't scared," he said with some doubt. "I'm a big boy."

"I know you are," Lisa reassured him. "But you still shouldn't be by yourself."

"I'm gonna go play football with Steve and Teddy. Then I won't be alone. But..." Mikey lowered his head.

"What's wrong, buddy?" Rodney asked.

"I can't find Butterscotch. I looked everywhere for him. He has to be here because he never goes outside. Mom said that Butterscotch doesn't have claws, so he can't go outside. Or mean animals might hurt him."

"Well, maybe he found a way out," Rodney said. "I'll go take a look and see if I can find him. Okay?"

"Okay."

"And in the meantime," Lisa said, "why don't you and I have a snack?"

"Alright!" Mikey agreed. "Punch and potato chips!"

"Punch and potato chips it is."

When Jermaine got home from work, he plopped down on his leather ottoman and started to Google the office of Dr. Alec Wilde. Alec Wilde. Wasn't that the cat who had gotten busted for being drunk on the job? After two rings, Alec himself answered.

"Hello, Dr. Wilde. My name is Jermaine Barrison. I'm a teacher at—"

"Oh, yes, Coach Barrison!" Alec interrupted. "I hear great things about you. We have, uh, a mutual friend."

"I'm sure it's that 'mutual friend' who I'm calling about. I realize that this conversation may be thirty-three flavors of unethical, but I felt the need to reach you."

"Oh God, please tell me something hasn't happened to Donovan."

Rodney checked the shrubbery around the perimeter of the house, looking for Butterscotch. When he got to the rear of the house, he noticed that the door of the shed, located at the head of the driveway, was closed but unlocked. Just to be thorough, he opened the door, not expecting to find anything. He was disappointed.

"Dude, what the hell?"

On the packed stone floor, partially hidden under a bottom shelf, lay Butterscotch. Patches of missing fur were present along his coat, as if the hair had been ripped out. He had an agonized look on his face. His yellow-green eyes were open wide and his tongue was sticking out. His head and neck rested at an unnatural angle. Ants and flies were making their rounds on his body.

Rodney found a garbage bag and put Butterscotch in it. After wrapping the bundle up, he placed it in a closed plastic trash barrel used for lawn clippings.

Obviously, the cat had been placed under the shelf by someone. Maybe a stray dog had killed Butterscotch. Maybe a dog or some other animal had killed him, and he had been temporarily placed in the shed by Donovan or one of his parents.

Could Donovan have done this?

Rodney tried not to think of that possibility.

4:48 p.m.

Chet Harter had been working Ashtabula County (which borders Pennsylvania) for nine years. He liked his jurisdiction. The people here were nicer; friendlier; safer. Unlike some of those hicks down in the Ohio

Valley who might fire on you if you looked at 'em cross-eyed. Chet was glad that part of his career was long over.

Conservation officer was his title now, but Chet preferred the older term of *game warden*. On a typical day, he liked to end his shift by strolling along the pier of Lake Shore Park and randomly asking to see fishing licenses. This was a typical day, and a fisherman happened to be just ahead.

"Afternoon, son," Officer Harter said.

"Hi," the boy, who looked a bit out of sorts, responded.

"Any luck today?"

"Huh?"

"Have you caught a lot of fish today?"

"Oh. No. Not really."

"Well, how long have you been here?"

"I don't know. Twenty minutes. Four hours."

Okay, maybe *a bit out of sorts* wasn't the appropriate description. *What's that saying that kids use nowadays? Batshit crazy. Yeah, maybe that's the more accurate term.* In addition to making that quick analysis, Chet wasn't particularly fond of the way the boy was staring at his side-arm.

"Don't worry. I haven't had to use that thing in a long, long time. Mind if I see your license?"

The boy gave him his driver's license.

"No, son. Your fishing license." Chet glanced at the card. "Well, it's nice to meet you, Donovan. You do have a fishing license don't you?"

The boy named Donovan looked over the water with a blank expression on his face. "No. I didn't know I needed one," he said in a monotonous voice.

"Well, it may not be your lucky day fishing, but it is with me. You see, my shift has come to an end, I don't get paid overtime, and my wife is making pork chops for supper." At the top of Chet's love list were Pabst Blue Ribbon and Betty's pork chops (made just like they do in his hometown of McDowell, Kentucky). "So you might be able to see why I have such a hankerin to get home."

Blank expression.

"I reckon I won't write you a ticket. A simple warning will do."

Blank expression.

"Son, are you going to be okay going home?" Chet took another look at Donovan's driver's license. "You're a long way from Harbor Light. Must've taken you over two hours to get here."

Donovan then seemed to snap out of his trance. "Yeah. I'll be okay. It's just that...I haven't been feeling well."

"I don't think I've seen you around. Have you fished here before?"

"No. I've never been here. I just got in the car and drove. This looked like a nice place to stop and fish."

"Well, it is. But you need a license. Make sure you get one before you throw your line in the water again. Nowadays you can get a license online."

"Okay. Thanks for just the warning." He retrieved his card from the officer.

Chet watched as the boy gathered his things and walked down the path to his white Fusion. He didn't see Donovan place his tackle box on the front seat, next to his father's Glock 9mm. That would have made their encounter far more complex.

Chet Harter later testified that if he had it to do over, he would have asked the boy more questions in order to better ascertain his mental state. And on any other day, perhaps he would have done just that. Betty's pork chops, though…

Donovan recalled yesterday's conversation with Mr. Rabbit. It was time to do something about the foxes. He started his car and began his long trek home.

In Harbor Light, the sunny sky turned overcast.

6:50 p.m.

Joe, Nancy, and Mikey Marsden returned home from their dinner at the local Texas Roadhouse. They had waited for Donovan to join them for awhile before they'd left, but figured that he must have gotten a bite to eat elsewhere. The landline phone rang.

Although patient privacy laws were, in this situation, the least of Alec's concerns, both he and Jermaine agreed that it would look better if the latter reached out to the Marsdens. He told Alec that he'd contact him with any new information. After calling the Marsden line several times, he finally got an answer.

"Hello."

"Hi. Uh, Mr. Marsden?"

"Yes."

"Hi. This is Jermaine Barrison, Donovan's phys ed—"

"Yeah, Coach! Donovan speaks very highly of you. Thank you so much for all you've done for him."

"You're welcome. Actually, sir, I'm calling because I'm concerned about him. He hadn't been in school all week—"

"Yeah, yeah, he has the flu. I'm sure he'll be back to school on Monday. I don't know where he is now. Maybe he went to the game."

"The last few times I saw him, he seemed to be somewhat detached—"

"I'm sure it was just the onset of the illness."

"Okay, well, can you do me a favor, Mr. Marsden?"

"Joe."

"Can you do me a favor, Joe?"

"Sure."

"Could you please have Donovan call me when he gets in? Just for my own peace of mind. His phone seems to be turned off."

"Sure, but it could be pretty late. Tonight's the last regular game of the season. He may be out late celebrating if it's a win."

"That's fine."

When Jermaine hung up a moment later, he figured the conversation had gone about as well as expected; indifference from the father. He considered what he would do next.

Joe placed the phone back in its cradle and thought. He had gotten home today from work before Nancy, and subsequently had been the one who found the note from Rodney McAllister on the kitchen table. Joe wasn't particularly broken up about Butterscotch (one less mouth to feed). He didn't immediately suspect Donovan of doing it (who knows what cats get into; it could have been anything). And he had yet to tell Nancy and Mikey of Butterscotch's demise (why ruin a perfectly nice Friday evening?).

On a hunch, Joe went into his bedroom. About a year ago, he'd shown Donovan where the firearm was kept and taught him how to use the semi-automatic for home defense. He'd also made his son promise that he wouldn't tell Mikey about it or show it off to his friends. Joe turned on the closet light and lifted up some linens on the top shelf. The gun was missing.

Throughout Joe Marsden's counseling/therapy sessions, he would often times hear terms such as concern, worry, empathy, sympathy. Those were just words to him. But could he be feeling a little something right now? Could he be experiencing a bit of *concern* right now? He didn't know. What he did know, was that he should call the sheriff's department.

9:49 p.m.

Harbor Light beat Clyde, 28-10.

After the game, Moose Talbot didn't even bother to shower. He just packed his gear and went home.

Even though he was loosely affiliated with Farrah LaCroix's crew, he knew that she would never let him in her *inner circle*, if there even was such a thing. He knew that he wouldn't be invited to cruise the strip after the game. Oh, he fantasized about her. He'd jerked off to her Instagram photos plenty of times. But it was clear that there would never be a romance, or even a true friendship. She kept him around only when he could serve a purpose. Just like he'd served a purpose with that Marsden brat, holding him down while Farrah rammed a broomstick up his ass. Not that he had any sympathy for him. He'd never liked the little dick, anyway. As far as Moose was concerned, Marsden had gotten what he deserved. He just didn't want to get in trouble for it. A week had passed, so Moose figured he was in the clear.

Moose was home alone at the Talbot farm, which was located on Harbor Light's rural east side. The gentle rain had started to intensify. He was in the pole barn, tinkering with his rusted 2002 Chevy Cavalier. The long, sliding front door of the barn was wide open.

Moose took a sip of Gatorade, then lay down on the creeper and rolled under his car to change the oil.

He liked the sound of the rain.

What's that?

Moose thought he heard another song outside coming through the song of the rain. *Guitar? Some oldies tune?* It got louder. *Neil Diamond?*

"Who's there?" Moose shouted.

From under the car, he looked to his right, left, right again.

The music cut off and Moose reflexively jerked up, banging his head on the car's undercarriage. "Ouch! Damn!" He remained there for a moment, waiting for the stars to leave his head. He then rolled out from under his car and made his way to the front door. "Who's there?" he repeated.

"Hi, Moose."

Moose quickly turned around and from about ten feet away beheld—the Marsden kid? "What the hell are *you* doin here?"

"You stink, Moose," Donovan said. "I can smell your nasty ass from over here."

"What are you doin here!" He picked up a socket wrench that was laying on his car's engine block.

"What am I doing here? I forget…oh, I thought I'd stop by and give you some payback. Isn't that what Ted called it? I'm going to put you down…permanently… and I'm going to do it with my bare hands."

Not since he was a small child, when his father would take him behind the barn and beat his hind end with a strop, had Moose experienced this much fear. Maybe it was the audacity of the situation that threw him off. Here was this punk little kid, less than half his size, standing there cool and calm (although he looked like he didn't know what year it was), saying that he was going to kill him with his *bare hands*? It was that fear that prompted Moose to lunge toward Donovan with an overhand swing of the wrench.

Donovan dodged the blow, pivoted, and jumped on Moose's back. He barely managed to wrap his legs around the bigger boy's enormous girth. Then, he executed a flawless rear naked choke, with Moose's Adam's apple squarely in the crook of his left elbow. He reinforced the hold by cupping his own right bicep and placing that hand on the back of Moose's head.

Standing, Moose knew that he had only seconds to get this kid off him before he passed out. He swung the wrench to his left, managing only to strike his own shoulder. He then swung it to the right and felt it connect. A gash opened up on Donovan's forehead.

Moose dropped the wrench and drove Donovan backwards into a metallic cabinet. Again. Donovan maintained his hold.

Blackness closed in on Moose's head and he felt his knees buckle.

Donovan didn't know how much time had elapsed since they went to the floor, with the larger boy on top of him, and with the sleeper hold still firmly intact. Four minutes? Thirty minutes? Three hours? He did, however, know two things: he would never be assaulted again.

And Moose Talbot would never breathe again.

Earlier that evening, Alec and Emily Wilde were enjoying a homemade dinner of steak and shrimp, with baked potatoes, green beans, and fried apples. They had planned on watching a movie on-demand afterward. She could tell that he was bothered, and she knew why.

"I know you're upset," she said.

"I just can't get it out of my head."

"I understand if you feel the need to go look for him."

"Maybe I'll just call Jermaine and see if he's found anything out."

Twenty minutes later, Jermaine picked up Alec at his front door.

After the game, off the field, Lisa and Rodney approached Chad Chandler and explained that they were worried about Donovan. He told them to wait for him while he took a quick shower and got his belongings together.

Now, they were driving around Sandusky, Harbor Light, and Huron, looking for Donovan's Fusion. Chad was driving. He was the only one of the three that had a car; and a license.

"Do you guys know of anyone who had it in for Donovan?" Chad asked. "Anyone who really pushed him hard."

"Why?" Rodney asked.

"Well, um…" Chad looked at Rodney and flashed a guilty smile.

"Rodney."

"Rodney. I'm sorry. Well, if Donovan has become violent…if he did kill his cat…if he's not thinking right…then maybe he's come up with some ideas. Some not-so-good ideas."

"I know he's had a couple of run-ins with Chucky Vasquez," Rodney said. "And he got in a fight with Ted Mullins." He looked back at Lisa.

"Don't forget about Farrah LaCroix," she said. "The queen bee of bullying."

"I don't think big Moose was a fan of his either," Chad followed up.

"What do you think we should do?" Lisa asked.

"I know where Moose and Farrah live," Chad said. "Maybe we'll just drive by and see if there's any trouble."

"Ted probably has a criminal record," Rodney said. "I could probably find his address online on my phone."

Sure enough, within a minute, he found Ted's address, who just happened to live nearby.

10:25 p.m.

Chad, Lisa, and Rodney crept along, driving slower as they got closer to 613 E. Howard Street. The rain made it difficult to read the numbers on the houses. Upon finding Angela Mullins's house, they inched by. As they did, they saw Ted in the living room through the large glass front window—wildly playing air guitar.

"What an idiot," Chad said.

"Well, he at least looks...safe," Lisa said with a smile.

Chad shook his head and chuckled. "Yeah. I guess we'll check out the Talbot farm now."

As the trio in the black Corolla registered to Jeff Chandler drove by, they didn't notice the white Fusion parked in an alley behind E. Howard Street—or the boy crouched behind the big oak in front of the Mullins home.

Jermaine and Alec were doing the same thing as the three kids, driving around the community looking for Donovan.

As soon as Alec stepped into Jermaine's Mustang, Jermaine informed him of what had happened earlier. Like Lisa and Rodney, Jermaine had gone to the game on the off-chance that Donovan would be there. He had run into an old friend near the concession stand, Deputy Jim Collins, who was on-duty. Jermaine had told Jim of his concern, and Jim had told Jermaine that there was an APB out on Donovan. A missing firearm was involved. Alec was almost as worried about his friend as he was his patient.

"I kept trying to call Art ever since you and I spoke this afternoon. It just goes directly to voicemail. It's never done that when I called him before."

"I can see why you're uneasy," Jermaine said. "I'm sure whistleblowers have to watch their every step. It's probably nothing. Maybe he just took an extended nap with his phone off."

"Why did you do it?"

"Do what?"

"Mentor Donovan. Help him out so much."

Jermaine took several breaths before answering.

"Donovan reminded me of my best friend when I was his age. His nickname was Mooky. He had a beautiful heart, but he got picked on. A lot. His dad took off before he was even born, and he never had a father figure at home. He got mixed up with a bad crowd. He died during a drug deal gone bad. I should have been there more for him. If so, then maybe his death could have been prevented." Jermaine paused. "I guess taking Donovan under my wing was my way of trying to atone for what happened to Mook."

"I'm sorry about that," Alec said. "I know all about atonement."

Up ahead, a white Fusion crossed Main Street onto Summit. Jermaine took a quick right and followed it. "Did you get a look at the driver?" he asked.

"No. But there doesn't look like there's anyone else in the car."

The Fusion seemed to speed up, as if the driver sensed that he was being tailed. At the next stop light, it took a left on yellow onto Carmen Avenue. Jermaine made the same turn as the light turned red.

The Mustang and Fusion were almost side-by-side, when the latter moved over into the next lane. As soon as it did, a gray Subaru pulled up to take its place.

"Damn!" Jermaine said.

Jermaine and Alec were locked in their lane and had to stop at the next light, while the Fusion drove on. Alec saw that it remained on Carmen.

When the light turned green, Jermaine said, "Time to let these horses run." He swiftly shifted two lanes to the right and put the pedal down. Alec felt his stomach rise as it reminded him of taking off in an airplane.

They pulled in one lane to the left and was flush with the Fusion at the next light.

Alec rolled his window down to get a better look.

A middle-aged woman responded with a smile.

"False alarm," Alec said.

"It may not be the last one of the night," Jermaine replied.

Donovan leaned against the big oak as he watched Ted Mullins foolishly play his make-believe guitar. He heard the whine of a Metallica tune drift through the sound of the rain.

Donovan reached into his right front jeans pocket and removed the Glock. Chambered a round.

As he did, Ted stopped flailing around. He seemed to notice something outside.

Donovan raised the gun and took Ted in its sights.

Who's the marksman?

"I'm the marksman."

Ted squinted his eyes and moved his head from side to side, slowly stepping closer to the window. Only ten yards separated the two of them.

Who's the sharpshooter?

"I'm the sharpshooter."

Donovan moved his right forefinger from outside the trigger guard onto the trigger.

The last thing in his life that Ted Mullins saw was a flash of light.

Donovan fired three rounds, each hitting Ted center-mass. The exit wounds showered the entire living room with blood, bone, skin, and other tissue. Ted dropped immediately.

11:02 p.m.

Jermaine and Alec were about to call it a night when Jermaine's phone rang.

"Hey, Jim, what's up?"

"Hey, Maine, I wanted to give you a heads-up," Deputy Jim Collins said. "I'm out on Clemson Road. Three kids found a body in a barn. The deceased is Daniel Talbot. Ring a bell?"

Jermaine thought for a second. "Moose Talbot?"

"That's him."

"What happened?"

"We don't know yet. Any reason why the Marsden boy would want to hurt him?"

Jermaine remembered the night of the homecoming dance. "Maybe."

"That's not all, Maine. We just got word that a boy named Ted Mullins was shot and killed at his home—"

"Ah shit, man. What's the address where you are, Jim? I'm on my way…"

Farrah LaCroix was having a bad night. The pic she'd posted earlier on Facebook (the one in her cheerleading uniform with her skirt hiked up to her rump), only had sixty-eight likes so far. The pic of Abby Hess (in her bikini at the indoor waterpark) had over a hundred likes. Bitch.

She and Chucky Vasquez were cruising around town. Chucky was driving. An occasional galpal of Farrah's (whom forensics later identified as Leslie Taylor) was in the back seat of the two-door sedan.

Drinking and driving was one of Farrah's and Chucky's favorite sports. She and the other girl split a pack of Mike's Hard Lemonade. Chucky stuck with Old Milwaukee.

They were now on the rural outskirts of Harbor Light, driving along Old State Road. Chucky noticed a pair of headlights distantly behind them. The rain had eased to a drizzle.

They were making final preparations for Farrah's Halloween costume party, slated for the following night. A who's who of Erie County cool kids would be there. John LaCroix would be out of town. Lots of fun to be had.

The car behind them (high-beams on) was getting closer.

"I still haven't made up my mind what I'm dressing up as," Farrah said. "A slutty nurse or a slutty pussy cat."

"As long as you're slutty," Chucky said.

"What are you dressing up like, Up-Chuck?"

Chucky thought for a second. "I think I'll go as a hobo."

"You already are a hobo. What the fuck is wrong with that guy?"

The car behind them was now practically on their bumper.

"Chucky, time for a little brake check," Farrah said.

Chucky, not wanting his old-school antique to get damaged, applied the brake, gently. The other car slowed down too, maintaining its proximity.

"Just pull over and let the douche pass," Farrah yelled.

They pulled over to the side of the road and came to a stop.

The other car did, too.

"I don't like this," the girl in the back said.

"Fuck it," Chucky said as he slammed on the pedal, spraying the prick behind them with stones.

He got up to fifty-five miles per hour; sixty-five; seventy-five. The other car stayed on their bumper.

"Faster!" Farrah screamed. "Faster!"

"W-w-whatthefuckman!"

"I don't like this," the girl in the back repeated.

The other car veered in the left lane and got beside Chucky's. The passenger-side window was down. Chucky's own window was rolled down. He got a good look at the driver.

"N-n-nofuckinway!"

The boy who they'd beat, wedgied, swirlied, and sodomized was smiling at them. He raised a gun. One shot was fired.

The bullet entered Chucky's right eye, passed through his head, and lodged in the door frame. It hadn't struck Farrah. She was struck with Chucky's blood and brain.

Chucky slumped over the steering wheel, and the car jerked hard to the left. After rolling over several times, it came to a rest upside-down in a field.

The fuel tank was ruptured.

Donovan stopped, got out of his car, and approached the other one. He fired into the undercarriage.

Again.

Again.

Again.

Suddenly, the car erupted into a ball of fire.

As he walked away, he heard a bloodcurdling scream. He didn't know if it came from Farrah or the other girl.

Didn't care.

11:18 p.m.

By the time Jermaine and Alec pulled into the Talbot farm, Lisa, Rodney, and Chad were finishing up giving their statements to law enforcement.

"Coach Barrison!" Chad yelled.

After a quick conversation with the cops and children, Alec (drawing on his experience with psychology) asked a question: "Look, kids, do any of you know of a meaningful place that Donovan may have gone to? Someplace really important to him."

"West Pier was a special place for us," Lisa said. "It meant a lot to him."

Chad nodded his head. "Yeah, we went fishing there a few times. He really likes it there."

11:41 p.m.

Deputy Jim Collins and an officer of the local PD led the caravan to West Pier. The deputy didn't think they would find Donovan there, but there was nothing wrong with following up on the doctor's hunch.

Law enforcement was thinned out tonight. In addition to two suspected murders, a tip had just come in about a crash off Old State Road.

When they pulled up, everyone saw Donovan sitting along the pier, with his back to them. Chad noticed that he was sitting in the same chair he always sat in when they fished. Lisa started toward the steps.

"Wait," Deputy Collins said. "Officer Jenkins and I will go up. He could be highly volatile."

"We don't even know if he's done anything," Alec said. "And if he did, and he is volatile, then maybe Lisa could calm him down."

"He's right, Jim," Jermaine said. "If he's high strung, he might go off if confronted by cops. Give Lisa a chance."

Jim Collins considered this. "Okay. But, Lisa, stay off to the side. Don't get between him and us. Alright?"

"Okay."

She walked up the ten short steps to the pier.

"Donovan."

Donovan turned his head, got up, and walked toward her. A solemn expression on his face.

"Guess I really messed up, huh?" he said.

"We'll get through it. Whatever it was."

"No. No, I don't think I can."

They both looked down for a few seconds.

"I'm sorry I was so mean to you. I haven't been myself lately."

"It's that damn drug, honey. Get off that and you can be your old self again."

"I hated my old self. I loved my new self. At least I thought I did."

"I love your old self; the sweet boy I fell in love with."

He looked at her left hand.

"The ring."

"I never did take it off." Tears streamed down her face.

"I love you, Lisa."

"I love you too, Donovan."

"Well. I guess it's time to go."

Donovan thrust his hand into his right front pocket.

"Stop!" Deputy Collins bellowed as he drew his side arm. "Don't move!"

Donovan turned toward the deputy, took a step back with his right foot, and quickly yanked his hand free. He was shot twice in the chest.

Lisa screamed.

Donovan released the item in his hand: his Super High Bouncy Ball. It bounced down the steps. He fell backwards off the pier and dropped eight feet to the shoreline, landing on his back. Lisa jumped down to him.

"Donovan!" She held him.

He looked at her.

She bawled.

"I wish...we could have tried again," he said.

And smiled.

And closed his eyes.

And died.

EPILOGUE

Ten months after the Occurrence in Harbor Light, B.J. Wentworth went to trial for various criminal activities. But not before being ousted as president and CEO of Braxton-Wentworth.

The off-label prescribing of Restor came to a halt.

Jermaine Barrison, who had started thinking of himself as the consummate bachelor, had a new girlfriend. It was getting serious. She had a little daughter, who got along wonderfully with Jamal.

Alec and Emily Wilde took a vacation to the Bahamas and renewed their vows.

Rodney McAllister missed his friend. Always would.

On his way to Columbus, Chad Chandler stopped by to say goodbye to Lisa Bailey. He wasn't going to Ohio State to play football. He was going to study sociology.

On the doorstep, she said, "Are you going to live in the dorms?"

"Nah. I'm moving into a rooming house on E. Twelfth."

"Sounds exciting." She fingered the ring on her left hand; figured she'd always wear it.

"I hope so. But not too exciting." They both laughed.

They hugged and said they'd keep in touch. He turned away, walked a few steps, and turned back toward her.

"I wish I could have known him before...everything," he said. "I think I really would have loved him."

She smiled.

"I know I did," she said.

If you liked the story, then please consider giving a review on Amazon. You can sign up for my newsletter for updates on new releases and more at EricKaple.com. Please keep in touch:

EricKaple@yahoo.com

www.facebook.com/EricKapleAuthor

Made in the USA
Monee, IL
29 April 2022